"You have a daughter,"

Hardy told her, his voice filled with awe.

"Is she okay?" Trish asked, struggling to sit up. "She's not too little, is she? She's early, not by much, but still, it would have been better if she'd waited."

"You're telling me," Hardy said dryly.

"Let me see her."

Hardy stripped off his flannel shirt and wrapped the baby in it. She snuggled in, looking as contented as if this weren't her first minute in the real world. He glanced at his watch. It was midnight on the dot. This little one had been in quite a rush to greet the new millennium.

Grinning, he placed the little sweetheart gently in her mama's arms. "Happy New Year, darlin'."

Dear Reader,

Happy Anniversary! We're kicking off a yearlong celebration in honor of Silhouette Books' 20th Anniversary, with unforgettable love stories by your favorite authors, including Nora Roberts, Diana Palmer, Sherryl Woods, Joan Elliott Pickart and many more!

Sherryl Woods delivers the first baby of the new year in *The Cowboy and the New Year's Baby,* which launches AND BABY MAKES THREE: THE DELACOURTS OF TEXAS. And return to Whitehorn, Montana, as Laurie Paige tells the story of an undercover agent who comes home to protect his family and finds his heart in *A Family Homecoming,* part of MONTANA MAVERICKS: RETURN TO WHITEHORN.

Next is Christine Rimmer's tale of a lady doc's determination to resist the charming new hospital administrator. Happily, he proves irresistible in *A Doctor's Vow,* part of PRESCRIPTION: MARRIAGE. And don't miss Marie Ferrarella's sensational family story set in Alaska, *Stand-In Mom.*

Also this month, Leigh Greenwood tells the tale of two past lovers who must be *Married by High Noon* in order to save a child. Finally, opposites attract in *Awakened By His Kiss,* a tender love story by newcomer Judith Lyons.

Join the celebration; treat yourself to all six Special Edition romance novels each month!

Best,

Karen Taylor Richman
Senior Editor

Please address questions and book requests to:
Silhouette Reader Service
U.S.: 3010 Walden Ave., P.O. Box 1325, Buffalo, NY 14269
Canadian: P.O. Box 609, Fort Erie, Ont. L2A 5X3

SHERRYL WOODS

THE COWBOY AND THE NEW YEAR'S BABY

SPECIAL EDITION®

Published by Silhouette Books

America's Publisher of Contemporary Romance

SILHOUETTE BOOKS

ISBN 0-373-24291-3

THE COWBOY AND THE NEW YEAR'S BABY

Visit us at www.romance.net

Printed in U.S.A.

Books by Sherryl Woods

SHERRYL WOODS

Whether she's living in California, Florida or Virginia, Sherryl Woods always makes her home by the sea. A walk on the beach, the sound of waves, the smell of the salt air, all provide inspiration for this writer of more than sixty romance and mystery novels. Sherryl hopes you're enjoying these latest entries in the AND BABY MAKES THREE series for Silhouette Special Edition. You can write to Sherryl, or—from April through December—stop by and meet her at her bookstore, Potomac Sunrise, 308 Washington Avenue, Colonial Beach, VA 22443.

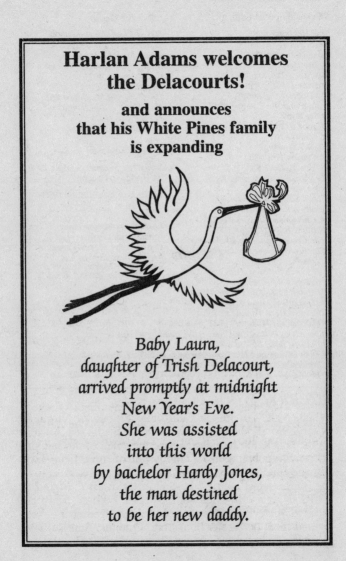

Harlan Adams welcomes the Delacourts!

and announces that his White Pines family is expanding

Baby Laura,
daughter of Trish Delacourt,
arrived promptly at midnight
New Year's Eve.
She was assisted
into this world
by bachelor Hardy Jones,
the man destined
to be her new daddy.

Chapter One

Country-western singer Laurie Jensen kept her gaze fastened on her husband as she sang her latest megahit at the End of the Road Saloon in Garden City, Texas. It was New Year's Eve and she and Harlan Patrick had taken over the bar and were hosting a private bash for the ranch hands from White Pines. The bar was packed with members of the Adams family, hands and their guests, but based on the adoring look on Laurie's face and the rapt expression on his, she and Harlan Patrick might as well have been all alone. Married for over a year now, they were still besotted with each other.

Hardy Jones watched with a disgusted shake of his head. It pretty much seemed to Hardy as if every male he knew was succumbing to love. First his boss and Laurie, then his buddy, Slade Sutton, and Laurie's assistant, Val. Watching the two couples tonight was giving him a first-class case of hives.

Not that he had anything against romance. Far from it. He loved women. He loved the delicate, feminine scent of them. After a long day with a herd of cows, just the soft, floral aroma of perfume was enough to kick his hormones into overdrive. The shimmering silk of long hair glistening in the sun was enough to conjure up thoughts of a fragrant curtain of curls teasing his flesh while making love. Beyond that, he appreciated the way a woman felt in his arms, the sheer wonder of all those lush curves.

Tonight, in a roomful of available, sensuous women, it seemed to him that irresistible temptation lurked everywhere. In fact it was a little worse than usual tonight because he was all alone and determined to stay that way.

Not five minutes ago a gorgeous redhead he'd been out with a few times had sidled up to him and whispered an indecent suggestion in his ear. He'd swallowed hard, fought off a surge of testosterone and turned her down.

"Not tonight, darlin'." It had taken an act of will to get the words out.

Looking disappointed, she'd run a vivid red fingernail along his cheek. His temperature had skyrocketed, but his willpower had remained firm.

"Another time, then?" she'd suggested.

"Count on it."

There had been others. From the moment he'd

walked into the bar, it had been like seeing his past flash before his eyes. Los Piños, where White Pines ranch was located, and Garden City were hardly major metropolises. He was pretty sure he'd met—if not dated—most of the single women in both cities at one time or another.

The truth was he'd made it a point to be thorough. At least half of the women here tonight were listed in his little black book, a virtual *Who's Who* of his bachelorhood. It seemed as if his buddies had invited every available female from a hundred-mile radius just to torment him.

As for his little black book, it was dog-eared and invaluable. He touched his pocket just to be sure it was safely tucked there. There were phone numbers in those pages for hot, sultry women who could make a man's vision blur with a kiss. There were numbers for all-American women who liked hiking and sports, for some who could cook a mouthwatering gourmet meal, and for some who could simply make him laugh. He'd slept with fewer of them than most people thought, but probably more than was wise.

Some he'd only been out with once or twice. A handful had lasted longer, until he'd started to notice the way their gazes lingered on the diamonds every time they strolled past a jewelry store. He'd crossed out any who were inclined toward jealous rages.

Yes, indeed, that little book was worth its weight in gold. The men in the bunkhouse at White Pines had offered him all sorts of incentives just to get a peek, but he kept it private. His social life was nobody's business but his own, even though an awful lot of people thought otherwise.

Of course, seeing so many of the entries gathered in one place tonight was a little disconcerting. He'd been walking a tightrope for the past couple of hours, exchanging friendly hellos and not much in the way of encouragement, trying to dodge some of the more persistent, clever females who weren't inclined to take no for an answer.

Ever since his arrival he'd been asked to dance to every song. Drinks had been sent over. A blonde named Suzy with long and very shapely legs displayed to mid-thigh had brought over an entire bottle of champagne. If he'd been in the market for a date, all of the attention would have been very flattering. As it was, it was making him jittery. His willpower was only so strong, and some of these women were doing their best to destroy it. Alcohol, cleavage, caresses—it was enough to test a saint.

But over the years Hardy had discovered that there were two days of the year on which a dedicated bachelor had to be on his guard: New Year's Eve and Valentine's Day. For 363 days a man could pretty much date whomever he pleased without worrying too much about the consequences. Pay a woman a little too much attention on either of those occasions, however, and a man could all but kiss his freedom goodbye. New Year's and Valentine's Day were meant for lovers and commitment, at least that's how the women he knew saw them.

At 29, Hardy still valued his freedom. Even surrounded by some of the most enthusiastic proponents of marriage in the universe at White Pines, he remained a staunchly determined holdout. He had his reasons. Good reasons. Reasons rooted deeply in the past, a past he never talked about and tried not to remember. He lived in the moment, not the past, and never the future.

He fended off another admirer, took a long swallow of the sole beer he'd been nursing, and tried to relax and get into the spirit of the party. It was hard to do when the only other bachelor not on the dance floor was the grizzled cook, who only had half a dozen of his own teeth left and forgot his plate with the fake ones more often than not. Sweeney was a whiz with a skillet, on the trail or off, but he wasn't much of a talker. He didn't seem to care much about women one way or the other.

"Hey, Hardy, what's your New Year's resolution?" Slade Sutton shouted across the bar, his arm wrapped tightly around the waist of the petite woman with him. "Aren't you creeping up on thirty? Is this the year you're finally going to let some lady catch you?"

Hardy scowled at the teasing. "Not a chance, Sutton. Just because you've got the prettiest woman in Texas by your side these days doesn't mean the rest of us intend to fall into that trap."

The very recently wed Val Sutton regarded Hardy with feigned indignation. "And just what is wrong with marriage?"

Hardy pretended to think really hard. "Let me see if I can count that high."

"One of these days," Slade taunted, "you are going to fall so hard you'll knock yourself out."

"Never happen," Hardy insisted.

"If you had a woman, you wouldn't be sitting all alone at the bar looking pathetic on New Year's Eve," Slade persisted. For a man who'd taken his own sweet time acknowledging how he felt about his new wife, Slade seemed awfully eager to see Hardy follow in his footsteps. He had all the fervor of a recent convert.

"I guess you've missed all the women who've been over here tonight. Val must have put blinders on you," Hardy retorted.

"Watch it," Val warned. "I may be little, but I pack a mean punch."

Hardy grinned at her. She was a spirited little thing. All woman, too. He fondly recalled all the times she'd sashayed around the ranch on outrageously spiked heels just to catch Slade's attention. The other hands had appreciated it, even if Slade hadn't.

"Oh, if only I'd seen you first," he said with an exaggerated sigh that was only partly in jest. Val was a keeper, all right. Even he could admit that. If he'd been a marrying man—and if it hadn't been so plain that Val fit with Slade and his daughter, Annie—Hardy might have made a pass at her when she'd first turned up at White Pines.

"One date with me and you'd never have settled for a broken-down cowboy like Slade," he told her.

She gave him a thorough once-over, then turned to her husband and did the same. When her survey ended, she regarded him with exaggerated sorrow. "Sorry, Hardy. Slade's the man for me, has been ever since I first laid eyes on him."

"Yeah, we all noticed that," Hardy conceded. "Took him a long time to catch on, though. He must be real slow."

"Since it's New Year's Eve, I'm not going to take offense at that," Slade retorted. "But I may make it my personal mission this year to see to it that you're the next White Pines bachelor to fall. If the word just happens to get out to Harlan Adams that you're looking to settle down, he'll take a personal interest in seeing you married. The man's got quite a success rate. Now that his son Cody and grandson Harlan Patrick are running the ranch, the old man's got a lot of time on his hands to dedicate to matchmaking. He's made it a full-time hobby."

Hardy shuddered, a reaction he didn't have to feign. "I take it all back," he said quickly. "Just stay the heck away from my love life—you and Harlan."

He'd already resolved to start the millennium by sampling as many women as he possibly could. Playing the field suited him just fine. He figured his life couldn't get much sweeter. A new woman every night pretty much kept boredom at bay. He played fair with every one of them. Treated them like queens. Respected them. Laid his cards on the table right up front, too, so they wouldn't go getting ideas that would result in hurt down the road.

Yet it never ceased to amaze him how many of those same women—smart as whips, most of them—could ignore what a man said when it didn't suit them. They seemed especially deaf on a night like tonight.

Yes, indeed, New Year's Eve was a marital minefield, and Hardy had no intention of having his firm resolution to remain a bachelor blown to bits.

He checked his watch, saw that he had an hour to spare before the clock struck midnight, then slid off the barstool. "Think I'll be heading home," he announced.

"Hey, it's not even midnight," Slade said. "You turn into a pumpkin if you stay out too late?"

"Maybe I've got a hot date waiting," he retorted, wishing it were true. As it was, he intended to get the best night's sleep he'd get until February fourteenth.

Famous last words.

Trish Delacourt was on the lam.

She had planned to be tucked away in a cozy little bed-and-breakfast with a fireplace in her room on New Year's Eve. She had it all picked out. She'd made the reservation the minute she'd seen the brochure. Her father, who had standing accounts in every luxury hotel in the world, would never think to look for her in some stranger's home.

And Bryce Delacourt was looking for her. She didn't doubt it for a minute. He was too controlling, too convinced he knew what was best for everyone around him not to be. He'd probably put half a dozen of his best private investigators on her trail the instant he'd realized she was gone.

Fortunately for her she was resourceful and her father was a workaholic. She had managed to sneak out of Houston while he was away on a business trip he'd sandwiched between Christmas and New Year's. The head start had been critical. Even a couple of days might keep her out of his reach as long as she kept moving and steered away from all the big cities where her father would be likely to concentrate his search. He was probably combing Dallas at this very minute, dead certain that she'd go somewhere where she could be pampered.

But at 25, Trish was tired of being the pampered, only daughter of an oil tycoon with four headstrong sons, who also treated her as if she were made of spun glass. She was tired of her father's condescending attitude toward her work. He acted as if the business she loved was no more than an indulgence, a cute little hobby to keep her occupied until she married someone suitable.

Of course he knew precisely whom she should marry. He'd handpicked the man for her, then all but coached him into proposing. For a time she'd been caught up in the whirlwind courtship, blinded by Jack's good looks, dimpled smile and easy charm. She had almost fallen in with her father's plan.

Then, with all the force of a bolt of lightning, her vision had cleared and she'd seen Jack for what he truly was—a weak-willed opportunist and a ladies' man. Heaven protect her from the type. If she ever dated another man, he would be ugly as sin, acerbic and completely unfamiliar with the legendary Bryce

Delacourt. For now, it was enough just to be out of Jack's clutches.

She'd plotted her escape like a prisoner scheming a breakout. Everything had been going swimmingly up until now. She'd felt the tension of the past few months sliding away. She'd felt in control of her own destiny, at least until a few minutes ago.

Unfortunately a couple of wrong turns and the weather had conspired against her. Just when she'd been counting her blessings, her car had skidded into a snowdrift and sputtered to a stop on a stretch of deserted highway in the middle of nowhere in West Texas. By her calculations, she was miles away from her destination. Images of that cozy little B&B were fading fast, and the new year was rapidly approaching. Snow was falling outside in a blinding swirl. Inside the car the temperature was dropping at a terrifying clip. Her hands and feet were already freezing.

And, unless she was very much mistaken, she was in labor. Apparently her baby was going to follow in her footsteps and not do anything right.

After another unmistakable contraction, she rubbed her stomach. "You know, kiddo, you could just settle down and go back to sleep. You don't want to come into the world in the middle of a blizzard. Besides, you're not due for two more weeks."

That news didn't seem to impress the baby. Trish's body seized with another contraction, hard on the heels of the last one. This one left her gasping for breath and near tears.

Angry now, she declared, "I am not having this

baby on the side of the road all by myself.'' She stared hard at her stomach. ''Understand?''

She was rewarded with another contraction. Obviously the kid had another of her traits: he or she wouldn't listen to reason, either.

Convinced by now that nothing she could say was going to change the course of events, she yanked her cell phone out of her purse and punched in the number for the State Highway Patrol. A blinking red light on the phone reminded her that in her haste to leave Houston and stay one step ahead of her father's detectives, she hadn't taken the time to charge the battery. The phone was dead.

''Stupid, stupid, stupid,'' she muttered, tossing the useless phone on the floor. How could a woman who'd bought, built up and sold her own business for a tidy profit—the last without getting caught by her father—be so dumb?

''Now what?'' she asked, not really expecting an answer. She was fresh out of ideas and, goodness knew, there was no one else in sight.

A quick survey out the window was not reassuring. There wasn't a house or a gas station within view. The last road marker she'd seen had been for Los Piños, fifteen miles away. Too far to walk even under the best of conditions.

The name of the town triggered a memory, though. One of her father's business associates lived in Los Piños, all but owned it from what she could recall.

Jordan Adams was head of a rival oil company. He and Bryce Delacourt had been friendly competitors for years. The one honorable man he knew, her father always said. They'd even been fishing buddies for a time when Jordan had lived in Houston, and they continued to trade tall tales about the one that got away. They still got together from time to time at business functions and at fishing lodges, where no wives were allowed.

Trish had no doubt that Jordan and his wife would come to her rescue, if only she could figure out some way to contact them. Unfortunately she also had a hunch that if he were even half the straight arrow her father described, Jordan would blab her whereabouts to her father the first chance he got. With the circumstances getting more desperate by the second, she was almost willing to take that risk.

"Why here?" she asked, gazing heavenward for answers that weren't forthcoming here on earth. "Why now?"

As if in response to her murmured questions, headlights cut through the pitch-black darkness. In such wide-open spaces, there was no way to tell just how far away they might be. She had to act and act quickly. There was no time to worry about the dangers of attracting a stranger's attention when she was all alone in the middle of nowhere. She needed help. She had to take her chances. Her baby's life was at stake. She'd already made a lot of sacrifices for the child she was carrying. This could be the most important one of all.

She jabbed frantically at the button to turn on her blinking hazard lights, then awkwardly heaved herself out of the car to signal to the oncoming driver.

Her feet skidded on the icy road and she clung to the car door to keep herself upright. More cautious now, she managed to slip-slide her way into the middle of the road, waving frantically, praying that the driver had at least a smidgen of the Good Samaritan in his soul.

At the last possible second what turned out to be a late-model, fancy pickup swerved, then skidded to a halt. The driver emerged cursing a blue streak. He ate up the distance between them in three long strides. Naturally he didn't slip. In fact, he didn't even seem aware that the ground was six inches deep in fresh snow on top of a sheet of slippery ice. She had to admire his agility, if not his choice of vocabulary.

When he was practically toe-to-toe with her, he scowled down, looking as if he would like very much to shake her. "Lady, are you out of your mind? I could have killed you."

Trish gazed up into eyes blazing with anger and what she hoped was at least a tiny hint of worry. Hoping to capitalize on that concern, she opened her mouth to explain her urgent predicament, but before she could, another wave of pain washed over her.

To her chagrin, she crumpled to the ground, right at the feet of the most gorgeous man she'd ever seen. If she hadn't been panting so hard, she might have sighed, maybe over him, maybe over the indignity of it all. Her only consolation was that, like Jack, this guy probably had women fainting at his feet all the time.

Chapter Two

"What the devil?"

Hardy dropped to his knees, oblivious to the biting cold wind and the six inches of wet snow that had made driving treacherous. What had happened to the woman? Had he hit her after all? Or was she some sort of insurance scam artist who was only pretending to be injured?

Or maybe just a nut case with a death wish? After all, she had planted herself directly in front on his oncoming truck on an icy road, all but asking him to run her down.

Whatever she was, at the moment she was clutching her stomach and writhing in pain. No matter which way he looked at it, that was not a good sign. If she was faking it, she was doing a really fine job of it. He was certainly buying it, and he was about as cynical as any man could be.

"Miss, are you okay?" he asked, gingerly brushing silky, blond hair back from a face streaked with tears. He couldn't quite bring himself to try to slap her back into consciousness.

"Come on now, darlin', wake up for me."

Finally, wide, blue eyes fluttered open, then promptly glazed over with unmistakable pain. Any lingering doubts he'd had about her faking it vanished.

"Are you okay?" he asked again, conducting a quick visual survey to try to determine if there were any cuts or broken bones.

"No, dammit, I am not okay," she snapped.

The words were ground out between panting breaths that might have been alarming if he hadn't just noticed the size of her swollen belly. How he could have missed it was beyond him. Maybe he'd been too entranced by that delicate, angelic face of hers, too distracted by the tears that smudged her cheeks. He cursed his ingrained tendency to get all caught up at the sight of a pretty woman and lose control of his common sense. He had a feeling the occasion called for really clear thinking. A pregnant woman in pain and flat on her back in the snow was not a good thing.

"You're having a baby," he said in a bemused tone, which was not exactly the brilliant observation of a man who'd gotten a firm grip on reality.

"Great deduction, Einstein," she said, clearly not impressed with his quick wit.

He continued to grapple with the implications. "Here?" he asked uneasily. Surely she wasn't in labor. Surely she'd just slipped and landed a little too hard. This wasn't the time or the place to be having a baby, and he definitely wasn't the right person to expect to assist in the delivery.

"Not if someone would get me to a blasted hospital." She glanced around in an obviously exaggerated search of the barren landscape. "Looks to me like you're elected, cowboy."

Sweet heaven, it was every bit as bad as he'd feared. She didn't seem any more overjoyed about the circumstances than he was. In fact, underneath that smart-mouthed sass of hers, she was probably scared to death. He couldn't say he blamed her. He was bordering on real alarm himself.

"Well, are you going to stand here all night or are you going to do something?" she demanded, rubbing her belly.

The movement of her hand all but mesmerized him. He'd never felt a baby move inside a woman before, never thought he wanted to, but for some reason he had to fight an urge to do so now. His willpower, already tested to its limits tonight, was called into play to restrain him from covering her hand with his own. As he struggled with himself, she scowled.

"Wake up," she snapped. "You aren't drunk, are you?"

"Stone-cold sober," he assured her. More was the pity. If he'd had more than one beer, he'd still be in Garden City, a long way from this woman and her problem.

"I hate to rush you, but I really think we need to get going," she said with renewed urgency. "Unless you'd like to loan me your truck and let me go on my own."

"Nobody drives my truck," he said tersely.

"Why am I not surprised?" she muttered. "Then how about we hit the road, cowboy? This situation is only going to get worse with time."

Her cheeks were damp with tears, which she brushed at impatiently. Clearly, she wasn't used to having to count on someone else, and even more clearly, she didn't like it.

Although in a practical way he could see her point, Hardy was not overjoyed with the plan. Tears rattled him. He hated to see anyone or anything in pain. And the mere thought of babies gave him hives almost as severe as the thought of marriage. He sincerely regretted being so anxious to flee the End of the Road Saloon. Normally cool and calm in a crisis, for some reason he couldn't seem to snap into action the way the situation required. No wonder she was losing patience.

"Where's your husband?" he asked, aware that he sounded just a little desperate. It was clear enough that the man wasn't close enough to help them out of this jam.

"No hus...band." She bit the words out between gasps.

Before he realized what she intended, she seized his hand in a grip that an ex-rodeo star like Slade

Sutton would have admired. There wasn't a bull on the circuit that could have thrown anyone hanging on that tightly. Hardy gently tried to extricate his fingers.

It was finally beginning to sink in that he had two choices: he could turn around and drive her to the hospital in Garden City or he could deliver the baby himself right here on the side of the road.

Over the years he'd delivered his share of calves and foals. He supposed he understood the rudiments of giving birth to a baby, but it seemed like an awfully personal activity to engage in with a complete stranger, especially one who was eyeing him as balefully as if he were the one responsible for her being in this predicament.

He figured this was no time for asking all the million and one questions that occurred to him, such as what she was doing out here all alone with a baby due any second. Terrified that the decision might be taken from him, he reached down and scooped the woman into his arms.

"Don't panic," he soothed. He figured he was panicked enough for both of them. "I'll have you at the hospital in no time."

"How far is it?"

"Not far," he reassured her. Too blasted far, he thought. Contractions as hard and fast as she was having them were not a good sign. Even he had sense enough to recognize that.

"Don't push," he cautioned as he settled her into the cab of his truck. "Whatever you do, don't push."

"Easy for you to say," she muttered, clinging to the door with a white-knuckled, viselike grip as another contraction washed over her.

Hardy leaned down and gazed into her eyes. "Sweetheart, you are not going to have this baby in my truck." It was part reassurance, part command. Apparently the baby didn't get the message, because a scream ripped from the woman's throat.

"Oh, my God, the baby's coming." Tears streamed down her cheeks, unchecked now, as she gave in to panic. "Do something. Please."

Hardy sucked in a deep breath of the chilly night air and reached a hasty conclusion. Like it or not, he was about to be midwife to this woman's baby. He touched her cheek with a soothing caress, trying not to notice how soft it felt to his callused fingers. She'd already proven beyond a doubt just how much trouble she could bring into a man's life. The last thing he needed was to be attracted to her. This was about helping her out of a jam, nothing more. He'd get this over with, deliver her to the hospital and wash his hands of her. It sounded like a sensible plan to him.

She turned those huge blue eyes of hers on him, blinking back a fresh batch of tears. "Help me, please."

The plea cut straight through him and propelled him into action.

"Shh," he whispered. "It's going to be just fine. I'll just spread a couple of blankets on the seat here so you'll be more comfortable, and we'll get this show on the road."

"Do you have any idea what you're doing?" she asked hopefully, struggling to stretch out in the cramped confines of the pickup.

"Enough," he promised. Calves, foals, babies. Nothing to it, he reassured himself. Just concentrate and help nature along.

After that, everything happened so fast he could hardly catch his breath. The next thing he knew, he was holding a tiny baby girl in his arms. She was screaming her lungs out, but she was the most beautiful sight he had ever seen. Tiny fingers and toes, every one of them perfect. A swirl of soft brown fuzz on her head. Eyes as blue as her mama's.

Amazing, powerful, unfamiliar feelings swept through him. He felt exhilarated, even more satisfied than he ever had after rambunctious sex. He had a hunch nothing he ever did would match the experience he had just shared with a woman he was never likely to see again.

He gazed into her anxious eyes. "You have a daughter," he told her, his voice filled with awe.

"Is she okay?" the woman asked, struggling to sit up. "She's not too little, is she? She's early, not by much, but still it would have been better if she'd waited."

"You're telling me," Hardy said dryly.

"Let me see."

"In a second. Let me clean her up a little, get her warmed up in something comfortable. Not that I'm any expert, but she looks just about right to me," he reassured her.

He stripped off his flannel shirt and wrapped the

baby in it. She snuggled in, looking as contented as if this weren't her first minute in the real world. He glanced at his watch. It was midnight on the dot. This little one had been in quite a rush to greet the new millennium.

Grinning, he placed the little sweetheart gently in her mama's arms. "Happy New Year, darlin'."

Hardy had a feeling it was going to be a long, long time before he got this New Year's out of his head. Next year he might even break tradition and have a date. Surely a date couldn't complicate his life any more than this stranger had.

"Oh, my God, she's beautiful," the woman whispered, then glanced at him. "Isn't she the most beautiful baby you've ever seen?"

"A real knockout," he concurred. "Now what say we bundle the two of you up and get you to the hospital?" He regarded her worriedly. "Sorry about the accommodations, but you'll have to sit up and hold the baby. Think you'll be able to?"

She nodded, her gaze never leaving her baby's face. She had to be uncomfortable, but with his assistance she struggled into a semi-upright position, then settled the baby in her arms.

When he was satisfied that she and the baby were as comfortable as they could be, Hardy eased the truck back onto the highway, turned around and headed toward Garden City. Although the condition of the roads required his full attention, he couldn't keep his gaze from straying to his companions. After a few, slow-going miles, both of them fell asleep, clearly exhausted by the whole ordeal.

Hardy, however, felt as wired as if he'd just downed a full pot of Sweeney's coffee. Normally he liked to tune in a country music station while he drove, but he didn't want to risk waking either mother or baby, so he hummed quietly. Christmas carols seemed oddly appropriate, so he went through a whole medley of them.

He calculated the time it would take him to get to the hospital, glad that his grown-up passenger wasn't awake to notice just how far away it was and just how big his lie had been when he'd told her before the birth that he thought they could make it. It had taken him better than half an hour to get from the party to where he'd been intercepted. The roads were worse now. Aware that he was carrying precious cargo, he was creeping along even slower than he would have been normally.

It was nearly one by the time he saw the lights of Garden City, another fifteen minutes before he saw the turnoff to the hospital. All that time and there hadn't been a peep from either of his ladies. He regarded them worriedly as he drove to the emergency entrance. What if they weren't okay? What if he'd done something wrong? What if the mama was bleeding to death? What was wrong with him? He should have driven faster, found a phone and called for help, something.

The roads around the hospital had been sanded. Even so, with the snow still coming down, the truck skidded when he tried to stop behind an ambulance, barely missing the back bumper of the emergency vehicle. Hardy bolted from the cab. Perfectly aware that he was acting a little like a crazy man, he raced into the emergency room shouting for help.

A nurse came flying out of a cubicle in the back, followed by a familiar face. He'd never been so glad to see anyone in his life as he was to see Lizzy Adams-Robbins, daughter of Harlan Adams and, far more important, a full-fledged doctor.

"What on earth?" she said when she saw him. "Hardy, what's wrong? Has there been an accident? You were at the White Pines party, weren't you? Did somebody get hurt?"

"Outside," he said. "My truck. A woman and a baby." For a man known for his glib tongue, he was having serious trouble forming sentences.

"Is the baby sick?" she asked, already moving toward the door at an admirably brisk pace.

"Newborn," he said, then drew in a deep breath and announced, "I delivered her."

Lizzy stopped and stared. So did the nurse who'd been running alongside.

"You delivered a baby?" Lizzy echoed. "Where? Why?"

"Just help them. Make sure they're okay," he said. "Don't you need a stretcher or a wheelchair or something?"

"Got it," the nurse said, grabbing a wheelchair.

Lizzy raced past him. Outside, they found the baby squalling and her mama just coming awake. Hardy helped Lizzy get the two of them into the wheelchair, then stood back as she whipped them inside.

Suddenly feeling useless, Hardy stayed where he

was. He sucked in a deep breath of the cold air and tried to calm nerves that suddenly felt strung tight as a bow. It was over now. The woman and her baby were in the hands of professionals. He could go on home, just as he'd planned.

But for some reason he couldn't make himself leave. He moved the truck to a parking space, then went back inside. He grabbed a soda from a vending machine, then settled down to wait for news.

He watched the clock ticking slowly, then stood up and began to pace. There was no sign of Lizzy or the nurse. Seconds ticked past, then minutes, then an hour.

Hardy was just about to charge into the treatment area and demand news, when the nurse returned.

"Everybody's doing fine," she assured him. "They've checked the mother and the baby from stem to stern and there are no complications. You did a great job, Dad."

Hardy started at her assumption. "I'm not the father," he informed her quickly. "I don't even know the woman."

The nurse didn't seem to believe him. She regarded him with amused skepticism that suggested she recognized him and that she'd heard tales about Hardy Jones. Since he'd dated quite a few people on staff at the hospital, it was entirely possible she had.

"Really," he insisted. "I found her by the side of the road. Her car had skidded into a snowdrift."

"Whatever you say."

"No, really. I'd never seen her before tonight."

She grinned. "Young man, you don't have to convince me. I believe you." She winked. "Of course, I also believe in the tooth fairy and Santa Claus."

Hardy sighed. Word of this was going to spread like wildfire. He could just imagine what the rumors would be like by morning. He'd never live it down.

"I have some paperwork here," the nurse said. "If you'd just fill out these forms for me, I'd appreciate it."

His frustration mounted at her refusal to take his word for the fact that he didn't know the woman in the back room. "I can't help you. I don't know her. I don't even know her name. I don't know where she's from. I don't know what sort of insurance she has. Ask her."

"She's pretty well wiped out," the nurse said.

"Then look in her purse. She probably has ID in there, an insurance card, whatever you need."

"I can't go through her purse," the nurse retorted with a touch of indignation. "I just thought, given your relationship, that you could provide the necessary information."

"There is no relationship," Hardy said tightly. "None. What about that word don't you understand?"

The nurse withdrew the papers with a heavy sigh. "They're not going to like this in the billing office."

Hardy whipped his checkbook out of his back pocket. "How much?"

The nurse blinked. "What?"

"I asked you how much. I'll write a check for it."

"I don't know the charges, not yet. She'll be here overnight at least. There will be routine tests for the baby."

"Then give me something to sign and send me the bill."

"You said you don't know her."

"I don't, but I wouldn't want your precious paperwork messed up. Just send me the bill, okay?"

The bright patches of color on the nurse's cheeks suggested embarrassment, but she popped some papers in front of him, anyway. Hardy signed them all. He knew, even as he scrawled his signature in half a dozen places, that he was dooming himself. After all, what kind of fool would pay for the hospitalization of a woman he didn't even know? Obviously everyone was going to jump to a far different conclusion.

Well, so be it, he thought as he jammed his checkbook back in his pocket and headed for the exit. What was it they said? No good deed goes unpunished. Between his reputation and his bank account, it looked as if he were going to take a real hit.

Then he thought of the baby and the sassy woman who'd been forced to trust him with their lives. What if they did cost him a few bucks? What if he took a little ribbing for a few weeks? It would pass soon enough.

And in the meantime he could remember forever that he'd been part of a miracle, the kind of unexpected miracle that a bachelor was unlikely to experience, the kind of miracle that assured a man of God's presence. What price could he put on that?

Chapter Three

The last thing Trish remembered was falling asleep, her baby in her arms, as the stranger rushed her to the hospital. She'd been exhausted, but she had never before felt such contentment, such an incredible sense of accomplishment.

She woke up to bright lights and chaos as three people swept her from the truck, wheeled her into the emergency room, then took her baby from her arms and clucked over her bravery. Once she was inside, there was no further sign of her reluctant hero. He vanished just as quickly as he'd appeared earlier. She hadn't even had time to thank him properly, to apologize for the grief she'd given him.

No one seemed to stay still long enough for her to ask a single question. Finally she latched on to the sleeve of a pretty, dark-haired woman whose bedside manner had been gentle, cheerful and briskly efficient. She read the name printed on her tag: Lizzy Adams-Robbins, M.D.

"Doctor, is my baby all right?" she asked. "She was a couple of weeks early, and I was in the middle of nowhere when she decided to come. The man who helped was wonderful, but he wasn't a doctor..." She realized she was babbling but she couldn't seem to stop.

"Your baby is perfectly healthy," the woman assured her. "She weighed in at a respectable seven pounds, three ounces. Terrific lung power. Despite the circumstances of her untimely arrival, I'd say everything turned out just fine."

Trish remembered the baby's wails and couldn't help smiling. "She already has a lot to say for herself, doesn't she? No wonder she was so anxious to get here."

The doctor grinned, then patted her hand sympathetically. "Right this second you may find that charming, but take it from me, you won't feel that way a week from now when she's been waking you out of a sound sleep a couple of times a night. By the way, have you decided on a name for her?"

Trish hadn't given the matter of naming the baby a lot of thought. Despite the increasing size of her belly, the routine of prenatal visits and regular kicks from an active baby, she had somehow gotten the idea that she had forever before she had to decide on anything as important as a name. She'd been too busy trying to plan her escape and steer clear of her father, who was dead set on having her marry the baby's father.

Even now with the baby a reality and the future uncertain, she still knew with absolute certainty that she wouldn't marry Jack Grainger if he were the last man on earth. On the same day she'd found out she was pregnant, she had also discovered that he'd been seeing at least two other women—intimately—while he was supposedly engaged to her.

Even if those two pieces of news hadn't collided headfirst, she would have wriggled out of the engagement. She'd discovered that Jack bored her to tears, maybe because he was so busy with his other women that he hadn't had time for her. She suspected he hadn't been any more overjoyed by the prospect of marriage than she had been. He'd just been too much in awe of her father—or her father's fortune, more likely—not to go along with Bryce's plans for the two of them.

Very methodically she had gone about quietly selling her business to a friend who'd expressed interest in it. She'd put her furniture in storage and slipped out of Houston. She'd been heading west to start the new year and a new life...someplace, when she'd gone into labor. The fact that her daughter had arrived early did not alter her determination to move ahead with her plans, and they definitely did not include Jack or any of the Delacourts.

The baby was her responsibility, and she was going to do right by her. That started with giving her a name she could be proud of, honoring someone who deserved it. Certainly not Jack. Certainly not anyone in her own family, since they'd all been far more concerned about convention than about her well-being or the baby's. Assuming that the marriage was a foregone conclusion, her mother had pleaded with her more than once to rush the wedding so that her pregnancy wouldn't show. When Trish had made it plain that there was to be no wedding despite her father's wishes, her mother had been appalled.

"What will we tell people?" she had demanded.

"That your daughter had better sense than to marry a man she didn't love."

"What does love have to do with it?" her mother had asked, genuinely perplexed. "I thought the two of you got along well enough. Jack is suitable. You've known him for years now. He has a place in your father's company, the promise of a vice presidency after the wedding."

That, of course, had been Jack's incentive. She'd had none, not any longer. "I've only known the side of him he wanted me—wanted us—to see. I certainly didn't know about the other women."

Ironically, her mother hadn't seemed nearly as surprised or dismayed about that as Trish had been. "You knew, didn't you?" Trish had charged, stunned that her mother would keep something like that from her.

"There were rumors," her mother admitted, then waved them off as unimportant. "You know how it is. A handsome man will always have women chasing after him. It's something you get used to, something you just accept."

"True," Trish agreed. "The difference is an honorable man, a man who actually cares about his fiancée, doesn't let them catch him."

"You're being too hard on him, don't you think? He was just having a little premarital fling."

"Or two," Trish said, wondering for the first time whether her father's behavior was responsible for her mother's jaded view of marriage. As far as she'd known, her father had never strayed, but maybe she'd been blind to it.

"Never mind," Trish had said finally. "It's clear we don't see eye-to-eye on this. Bottom line, hell will freeze over before I marry Jack. I'm sorry, but you'll just have to get used to the disgrace of it, Mother."

Of course she hadn't. Straight through until Christmas Day, with Trish's due date just around the corner, Helen Delacourt had remained fiercely dedicated to seeing Trish and Jack married. Without informing Trish, she had even included him on the guest list for the family's holiday dinner. When he'd arrived, Trish had promptly developed a throbbing headache and excused herself. Even as she went to her room, she could hear her mother apologizing for her. If she hadn't already been planning to leave town, overhearing her mother's pitiful attempts to placate the louse would have spurred her to take off.

"Hey, where'd you go?" the doctor asked gently.

Back to a place she hoped never to set foot in again, Trish thought to herself. "Sorry. I guess my mind wandered for a minute. What were we talking about?"

"Naming your baby."

"Of course." She thought of the man who'd helped her. He might have been caught off guard. He might not have wanted any part of the crisis she had thrust him into, but he'd pulled through for her. She and her baby were fine, thanks to him. "Do you happen to know the man who brought me in?" she asked the doctor.

"Sure. He works at my father's ranch." She chuckled. "I've got to tell you I've never seen a man so relieved to get to a hospital in my life."

"What's his name?"

"Hardy Jones. I'm not sure where the nickname comes from. I've heard Daddy say it has to be short for hardheaded because he's resisted every single attempt that's been made to get him married off. You'd have to know my father to understand how annoying he finds that. He's not happy unless he's matchmaking and he's not ecstatic unless it's paying off."

"Well, I certainly can't name the baby that," Trish said, disappointed. "Do I have to decide right now?"

"No, indeed. We'll need it before you leave the hospital, but it can wait. You take your time and think it over. Get some rest now. I'll be back to check on you later, and the nurses will bring the baby in soon so you can feed her."

Trish lay back against the pillows and let her eyes drift shut. The image that came to mind wasn't of her baby, but of the cowboy who'd delivered her.

"Hardy," she murmured on a sigh. A strong man

with a gentle touch. She could still feel the caress of his work-roughened hands as he'd helped her in one of the most terrifying, extraordinary, wondrous moments of her life. No matter what happened in all the years that stretched ahead, she would never forget him, never forget the miracle they'd shared.

"Hey, Hardy, I hear you're a gen-u-ine hero," one of the men taunted at the bunkhouse the next morning. Hardy grimaced and concentrated on spooning his oatmeal into his mouth.

"Yes, indeed, our boy has delivered himself a baby girl by the side of the road," another man said. "Is that some new technique of courting that I missed? No wonder I'm still crawling into a cold bed all alone at night."

"Oh, go to blazes," Hardy snapped, sensing that there was no let-up to the teasing in sight. He grabbed his coat off the back of the chair and stormed out of the bunkhouse.

It had been like this ever since the word of his good deed had spread at dawn. He'd barely crawled into his bed, when it had been time to crawl out again. Lack of sleep had left him testy. By the time everyone had come back in from their chores for breakfast, he'd been the nonstop subject of their good-natured taunts. Even the untalkative Sweeney had thrown out a sly comment while he'd dished up the oatmeal.

Outside, Hardy drew in a deep breath and tried to clear his lungs of the smoke that permeated the dining room.

"Hardy, could I have a word with you?" Cody Adams called out, poking his head out the door of his office and beckoning for Hardy to come inside.

Hardy walked over and followed his boss into the cluttered office, wondering what his boss wanted to discuss. For the last year or so Cody had let his son, Harlan Patrick, deal with the hands more often than not. Cody ran the business side of things, analyzing the market for beef on his computer, determining the best time to take the cattle to market, tracking down the best new bulls for breeding. Harlan Patrick knew the land and the herd. He knew which men he could rely on and which were capable, but lacked initiative. He and his father had arrived at a division of labor that suited them.

"Congratulations! I hear you delivered a baby girl last night," Cody said, proving right off that the conversation had nothing to do with ranch business. "Did a right fine job of it from what Lizzy tells us."

"Lizzy had no business blabbing," he grumbled. "I just did what had to be done. Dropped mother and child off at the hospital, and that was the end of it."

"I'm sure that's how you see it, but the new mama's mighty grateful. Lizzy phoned a little while ago and said she'd like you to come see her. If you'd like, take the morning off and drive on over to the hospital."

The very idea of seeing the woman again panicked him. He'd felt too much while he was delivering that baby—powerful, unfamiliar emotions that his bachelor's instincts for self-preservation recognized as way too risky. "I can't ask the men to take on my chores," he hedged, grasping at straws. "We're short, anyway, because a couple of the men aren't back from their holiday break."

"I'll pitch in," Cody said. "I still have a rough idea of how things work around here. Go on. Let the lady deliver her thanks in person. Get another look at that baby. Wouldn't mind getting a peek at her myself. Did you ever hear how my brother Luke delivered Jessie's baby, when she turned up on his doorstep in the middle of a blizzard?"

Oh, he'd heard it, all right. It was the stuff of Adams legends. Every man on the ranch had heard that story. He also knew how it had ended, with Luke and Jessie married. That ending was warning enough to him. He wasn't about to risk such an outcome by spending a minute more than necessary with the woman whose baby he'd delivered. He ran a finger around his collar, as if he could already feel the marital noose tightening around his neck.

"I've heard," he said tightly.

Cody chuckled at his reaction. "I suppose a bachelor like you would find that scary, seeing how they ended up married. Well, you go on over to the hospital just the same. Take your time. With so little sleep, you won't be much use around here, anyway. Besides, you deserve a break after what you went through last night."

No, what he deserved was to have his head examined, he thought as he reluctantly climbed into his truck and headed toward Garden City. He was asking for trouble. He could feel it in his bones.

As if the reaction at the ranch wasn't bad enough, he was greeted like a hero by the staff in the emergency room, too. The response made him queasy, especially since he'd dated quite a few of the admiring women in there at one time or another. Thanks to that paperwork he'd filled out, he figured half of them were speculating on just how close he was to the new mother. The other half were probably hoping this would make him more susceptible to the idea of marriage. He couldn't get out of the reception area fast enough.

Rather than going to the mother's room, though, he detoured to the nursery. An infant—female or not—was a whole lot less risk than a beautiful mama.

That's where Lizzy Adams found him, peering in at that tiny, incredible little human he'd brought into the world the night before.

"Amazing, isn't it?" she said, standing beside him to look through the glass. "I never get over it. One minute there's this anonymous little being inside the mother's body, and the next he or she is out here in the real world with a whole lifetime spread out before them. It surely is a miracle."

Hardy nodded, wishing he'd managed an escape before getting caught. "Yes, ma'am, it surely is."

"Are you here to see Trish? She's been asking for you. To tell you the truth, grateful as she is about your help last night, she's mad as spit that you agreed to pay her hospital bill. I thought I ought to warn you."

"I only agreed because that barracuda of a nurse panicked over the paperwork," he said defensively.

"Whatever. I'm sure the two of you will work it out."

"Maybe I'll wait to go see her, though," he said, seizing the excuse. "She's got a right sharp tongue when she's riled up. I wouldn't want to upset her."

Lizzy grinned at him. "Want to hold the baby first?"

Hardy was tempted, more tempted than he'd ever been by anything other than a grown-up and willing female. That was warning enough to have him shaking his head.

"I don't think so."

She regarded him knowingly. "You're not scared of a little tiny baby, are you?"

He scowled. "Of course not."

"Come on, then," she said, grabbing his hand and propelling him into the nursery. "You can rock her. Look at that face. You can tell she's getting ready to wail again. She's been keeping the other babies up."

Before he could stop her, Lizzy had him gowned and seated in a rocker with the baby in his arms. He stared down into those wide blue eyes and felt something deep inside him twist. Oh, this was dangerous, all right. If he'd been able to thrust her back into Lizzy's arms without looking like an idiot, he would have.

"She's beautiful, don't you think?" Lizzy asked, gently smoothing the baby's wisps of hair.

A lump formed in Hardy's throat. He was pretty

sure he couldn't possibly squeeze a word past it without making a total fool of himself. He nodded instead, rubbing the back of his finger along the baby's soft cheek. She was…amazing. It was the only fitting word he could think of. Since he'd never considered marriage, he'd figured fatherhood was a moot point. Holding this precious little girl in his arms, he was beginning to realize that he was actually sacrificing something incredible.

"Here comes her mama now," Lizzy said brightly. "Don't you two be fighting over her."

She beckoned to the woman who was gazing through the window. Hardy took one look at the baby's mama and wanted to flee. She was every bit as beautiful as he'd remembered, every bit as much of a shock to his system. If he hadn't been holding her baby, if Lizzy hadn't kept a hand clasped on his shoulder in a less-than-subtle attempt to keep him in place, if it wouldn't have been the most cowardly thing he'd ever done, he would have leaped up and run like crazy.

Lizzy made the formal introductions that had been skipped the night before, gave them both beaming smiles, then took off and left them alone, clearly satisfied by a sneaky job well done. Hardy awkwardly got to his feet, then gestured toward the rocker.

"After what you went through a few hours ago, you should be sitting down," he scolded.

Trish gave him an amused look, but she dutifully sat. He all but shoved the baby into her arms. For a moment, with her attention riveted on her daughter, neither of them spoke. Eventually she sighed.

"I still can't quite believe it." She looked up at him. "Thank you."

"No thanks necessary."

"You handled it like a real pro. Are you in the habit of delivering babies by the side of the road?"

"No way. This was a first for me. Can't tell you how glad I am that I didn't foul it up. What were you doing out on a lonely stretch of highway in a snowstorm, anyway?"

"Running away from home," she said wryly. "It's a long story."

And one she clearly didn't want to share. Hardy pondered why a woman in her twenties would need to run away from home. Was it that husband she'd said didn't exist that she was leaving? If so, getting to know her any better would just be begging for trouble. He twisted his hat in his hands, then asked, "Does that mean you're not from around here?"

"Yes. I'm just passing through."

To his surprise, her reply actually disappointed him. Because he wasn't wild about the reaction, he backed up a step. Entranced by the daughter, intrigued by the mother, he was likely to do something he'd regret. In fact, if he wasn't very careful, he might be crazy enough to suggest that she stay on just so he could sneak an occasional peek at that little girl growing up. The words might pop out despite his best intentions to steer as far away from them as possible from this moment on.

"Ought to be going now," he said in a rush.

She reached out a hand, but he was too far away for her to make contact. The gesture was enough to bring him to a halt, though.

"Oh, no you don't," she said firmly. "You and I need to talk."

"About the bill," he guessed, based on Lizzy's warning. "Don't get all worked up over it. I was just trying to keep the nurse from having apoplexy. You know how hospitals are about their forms these days."

"Oh, I'll admit that threw me, but I figured out what had probably happened. It's settled now. I've already explained to the billing office that the bill is my responsibility," she said. "No, what I wanted to talk to you about is more important."

Hardy regarded her warily. He didn't like the sound of that. "What's that?"

"The baby needs a name. I was hoping you could help me choose one. Something that would be special to you." Her gaze met his. "Your mother's name maybe."

Hardy froze at the mention of his mother, a woman who'd run out on him so long ago he could barely recall what she looked like. It wasn't a betrayal he was ever likely to forget, much less honor.

"Never," he said fiercely.

The fervent response clearly startled Trish, but unlike a lot of women who'd have taken that as a sign to start poking and prodding, she didn't pursue it.

"Another name, then. Maybe a sister or a girl you've never forgotten."

Hardy thought of the older sister who'd left home with his mother. Neither of them had ever looked back. He'd go to his grave resenting the fact that his mother had loved his sister enough to take her but had left him behind.

Then he considered the long string of woman whose memories lingered. None were important enough that he wanted to offer their names.

Finally he shook his head. "Sorry."

"Surely there's a girl's name you like," she persisted. "Or even a boy's name that we could change a little to make it sound more feminine."

He squirmed under the intensity of her gaze and her determination to pull him into a process that was by no means his to share. Naming a baby should be between a mother and a father. A stranger should have no part in it. But he recalled that she'd told him the night before that there was no father. Well, obviously, there was one, but he wasn't in the picture. That still didn't mean that Hardy had any business involved in this.

"Can't think of a single name," he insisted, hoping that would be the end of it.

"Well, then, I guess it will just have to be Hardy, after all."

He thought at first she was teasing, but he could see from her expression that she was flat-out serious.

"Oh, no," he said adamantly. "That's no name for a pretty little girl. Not much of one for a man, if you think about it. Comes from Hardwick, an old family name on my daddy's side. At least one boy in every generation had to be a Hardwick. Just my luck that I came along first in my generation. You would think after all those years of saddling poor little kids with that name, some mother would put her foot down and insist on something ordinary like Jake or Josh or John.''

''What were the girls in your family named?''

He chuckled as he thought of his cousins, every one of whom had been named after flowers. They'd viewed that as being every bit as humiliating as Hardwick. ''Rose, Lily, Iris,'' he recited, ticking them off on his fingers. He watched her increasingly horrified expression and kept going for the sheer fun of watching the sparks in her eyes, ''I believe there might even have been a Periwinkle a few generations back.''

Testing her, he said, ''How about that for your baby? I really loved hearing about old Peri. To hear my father tell it, she was ahead of her time, quite the feminist.''

Trish laughed. ''You're kidding.''

''About Peri?''

''About all of it.''

He held up a hand. ''God's truth. I swear it. Somebody, way back when, had a garden thing. Nobody who came after had the imagination to stray from the theme.'' He finally dared to look straight into Trish's eyes, which were sparkling with little glints of silver that made the blue shine like sapphires. ''Okay, forget Peri. What's wrong with naming her after yourself? Trish is a pretty name.''

''Short for Patricia,'' she explained derisively.

"It's a fine name, I suppose, but too ordinary. I want something that will make her stand out."

"Take it from someone whose name was a constant source of teasing, ordinary has its merits."

He paused for a minute, suddenly struck by a memory of the one woman in his life who'd been steadfast and gentle, his grandmother Laura. She'd died when he was only ten, but he'd never forgotten the warmth she had brought into his lonely life on her infrequent visits. She'd smelled like lily of the valley and she'd always had little bags of candy tucked inside her purse. She was the one person on his mother's side of the family who'd ever bothered to stay in touch.

"There is one name that comes to mind," he said, still hesitant to become involved in this at all. His gut told him that even such a tenuous tie to this woman and her baby was dangerous.

"Tell me," she commanded eagerly.

"Laura. It's a little old-fashioned, I suppose. It was my grandmother's name."

"And she meant a lot to you?" she asked, searching his face.

"A long time ago, yes, she did."

Trish's expression brightened then. "Laura," she said softly. "I like it."

Hardy liked the way it sounded when she said it. He liked the way her voice rose and fell in gentle waves. Even when she'd been snapping his head off during the baby's birth, there had been a hint of sunshine lurking in that voice.

He liked everything about this woman a little too

much. She and her baby were the type who could sneak into a man's heart—even his—before he knew what hit him. Just thinking that was enough to have him heading for the exit from the nursery.

"You're leaving?" Trish called after him, clearly surprised by the abrupt departure.

"Work to do," he said tersely, not turning around. "I meant to go a while back."

"Maybe I'll see you again."

"Since you're not from around these parts, I doubt it."

He hesitated, then turned and took one last look at the two of them, sitting in that rocker with the sunlight streaming in and spilling over them. He had a feeling that image would linger with him long after he wanted to banish it.

"I'm glad everything turned out okay," he said. "You all have a good life wherever you go."

Not until he was out in the hallway with the door firmly closed behind him did he begin to feel safe again.

Chapter Four

Trish had no idea what to make of Hardy Jones. He wasn't like any other man she'd ever known. He was brusque and tough one second, a little shy the next. As gorgeous and enigmatic as he was, she could imagine women falling at his feet, wanting to unravel the mystery of him. She had no intention of being one of them.

He'd done her a huge favor. She'd thanked him. There was no reason for their paths to cross again. In fact, he'd made it plain that he'd prefer that they didn't. Given some of the gossip she'd heard in the hallways about his active social life, she'd concluded he was a little too much like Jack. She certainly didn't need another man like that in her life.

After Hardy had gone, her doctor magically appeared in the nursery as if she'd been waiting just outside the door.

"So, what did you think of Hardy?" she asked.

It seemed to Trish that she posed the question a little too casually. Her watchful gaze suggested she was very interested in the answer. Alarm bells went off. Between her father and her big brothers, Trish had spent her entire life with overactive meddlers. She knew one when she saw one. She phrased her reply very carefully.

"He's very sweet, but he seemed nervous. He must be awfully shy around women, or is it just me?" she said, testing what she'd overheard about Hardy's womanizing.

The doctor's mouth gaped predictably. "Hardy, shy? That has to be a first. If you asked a hundred women around this part of Texas to describe him, I doubt there's one who would come up with that."

The doctor's description confirmed her worst fears. "You said you've known him for a while, Doctor. How would you describe him?" Trish asked curiously.

"Forget the 'Doctor,' okay? Call me Lizzy. I think we're going to be friends. As for Hardy, well, I'd have to say he's a hunk. The general consensus rates him as sexy, handsome and charming," she replied without missing a beat. "A real ladies' man. The word around here is that he can accelerate a pulse rate faster than a treadmill."

All the traits Trish had vowed to avoid in a man, she thought. It was strange, though. Obviously she had noticed that the man was gorgeous, that he exuded masculinity, but she'd been more struck by his gentleness, by his uneasiness around her. Not once had he tried to charm her. Of course, she doubted any man on earth would be inclined to flirt while delivering a baby, but what about today? Was she that much of a wreck that he hadn't even been inclined to try? And why did she find that so annoying? It was probably just some weird hormonal shift.

"I hadn't noticed," she said, aware that she sounded ever so slightly testy about it.

The doctor pulled up another rocker and sat down, clearly ready for a friendly chat. "I'm amazed," she said. "Flirting's as ingrained in Hardy as breathing. Are you telling me he never so much as winked at you?"

"Nope."

"Hmm. Isn't that fascinating?" Lizzy said. "No little innuendoes, no flattery, no sweet talk?"

"Afraid not." She grinned. "Of course, I have just had a baby. Not many men would flirt with a brand-new mother. What's he going to say? You look pretty good for someone who's just had a baby in my truck?"

"You don't know Hardy. The guys say..." She hesitated. "Well, never mind what the guys say. Let's just leave it that Hardy likes women. Correct that. Hardy loves women. Big, small, old, young."

Trish studied her intently. "Why are you telling me all this?"

"Just sharing information," Lizzy insisted. "In case you're interested."

"I just had a baby," Trish reminded her. "I'm passing through town. Why would I be interested?"

Lizzy shrugged, unperturbed by her response. "I just thought you might be."

Trish recalled what Lizzy had said about her father's matchmaking on Hardy's behalf. Obviously she shared the trait. It just seemed a trifle misplaced under the circumstances. "It hasn't occurred to you that I could have a husband somewhere?"

"No mention of one on your hospital forms," Lizzy said. "I checked."

Trish stared. "You didn't."

"Of course I did," Lizzy replied unrepentantly. "You have to admit that having a baby together—"

"He delivered the baby," Trish corrected impatiently. "We didn't have one together."

"Still, it had to be an incredibly intense moment. That's the kind of moment that creates an enduring bond, don't you think?"

Friendly chitchat was rapidly turning into advice for the lovelorn. Trish figured it was time to put a very firm stop to it. "Oh, no, you don't," she warned. "Stop it right there. Obviously you have your father's matchmaking tendencies. I am not in the market for a man. Hardy clearly wasn't the slightest bit interested in me. Even you have to realize that, since he didn't even bother to try to charm my socks off."

"But that's what makes it so interesting," Lizzy insisted. "For a man like Hardy not to flirt, for him to actually act all shy and tongue-tied around you, I think that's very telling."

"And I think you've been at the hospital too long without sleep," Trish said. "You're hallucinating."

"We'll see," Lizzy said, undeterred.

"Afraid not. As soon as I'm back on my feet, the baby and I will be moving on. I'll probably never see Hardy Jones again."

Famous last words.

Not an hour after she'd made her very firm declaration to Lizzy, Jordan and Kelly Adams appeared. Trish wasn't dumb enough not to realize that there was a connection, especially when they suggested she come and stay with them.

"We have lots of room, and you need to get some rest. Having a brand-new baby is exhausting. You'll need help, at least for a while," Kelly said. "Don't even bother making excuses. I'm not taking no for an answer."

"It's the least we can do for Bryce's daughter," Jordan added. "Your father…"

Before he could get the rest of the words out, Trish cut him off. "My father is not to know I'm here," she said firmly. "I can't come with you, unless you agree to that. If you feel you have to tell him, then I'll just take the baby and move on."

Kelly squeezed her hand and shot a warning look at her husband. "I'm sure you have your reasons, though I hope you'll reconsider. I'm sure he must be worried sick about you. In the meantime, we want you here with us. Isn't that right, Jordan?"

He looked uncomfortable with the promise, but he finally nodded. "It's your decision."

"By the way, how did you even know I was here?"

"Word travels fast in a small town," Kelly Adams said. "It's hard to get used to, if you've lived in the city most of your life."

"And in this family, word spreads like wildfire," Jordan added. "Never known a worse bunch of gossips. My father's the worst."

"Then you and Lizzy *are* related?" she asked, trying to reconcile the age difference.

"She's my half sister," he said. "We share the same impossibly nosy father. No doubt you'll meet him. He's chomping at the bit to get over here and get a look at you and the baby. With luck we'll be able to keep him away until you move into the house, but don't count on it. He's not a patient man."

"He's also looking for a new project," Kelly warned her.

Trish managed a wan smile. "I've heard about the matchmaking. Lizzy seems to have inherited the trait."

"Yes, well, I don't know about Lizzy, but he certainly does seem to have a flair for it," she said. "He did well enough by us."

Jordan frowned at her. "I'm the one who courted you, remember? My father had nothing to do with it."

Kelly patted his hand. "You go right on thinking that, sweetheart."

Trish was fascinated by the byplay between them. There was so much obvious affection, so much love.

Her own parents were not especially demonstrative. She'd assumed it was that way between all couples after many years of marriage. Obviously, that was not the case with Jordan and Kelly Adams.

He was a handsome man, a polished businessman with his well-trimmed hair and his fancy suit. He carried off the look of success with flair. Kelly, however, looked as if she'd just hopped off a horse and grabbed a ride into town with him. They both had to be in their forties, but while Jordan had a touch of gray in his hair and a few lines on his tanned face, Kelly was as vibrant and lovely as a girl. No one would have taken a quick look at them and guessed them to be a match. But judging from the way Jordan gazed at her, he adored her. And Kelly couldn't seem to keep her own gaze from straying to her husband every few seconds.

If only she could have fallen in love like that, Trish thought with a sigh. Instead, she'd fallen for a playboy with about as much substance as whipped cream.

Well, never again. Even if she stayed in the area for a few days or even a couple of weeks, she would do her best to avoid Hardy Jones. Rather than intriguing her, Lizzy's recitation of Hardy's attributes had solidified her determination to stay the heck away from him. And all of the hints that Harlan Adams might try to throw the two of them together were enough to make her skin crawl.

Realistically she couldn't take off in the next day or two, but she wouldn't hang around much longer than that. These people could plot and scheme and matchmake to their heart's content, but she was immune.

More important, in no time at all she and Laura would be far away. Hardy Jones wouldn't even be an issue once she'd found a new place to settle down. She'd been thinking New Mexico or Arizona, but Alaska was beginning to seem attractive. Or Maine. Any place that would put a few thousand miles between her and the growing number of people who seemed to think they knew just what she needed to make her life complete.

Hardy was constantly amazed at just how hot and sweaty a man could get when the temperature was barely above freezing. He and Harlan Patrick had been riding hard for most of the day, checking on the cattle to see how they'd done during the storm, making sure there was feed available, since most of the grazing land was still covered with a blanket of snow. All he wanted was a hot shower, a decent meal and sleep.

Instead, as he walked through the bunkhouse door, he was greeted by Harlan Adams.

"Hey, there, son, you're just the man I've been looking for."

In all the years he'd worked at White Pines, the owner had never sought him out before. Hardy regarded him warily. "Oh? Why is that?"

"Just wanted to add my congratulations to everybody else's. You did a fine thing the other night, helping out a stranger. Couldn't have been easy circumstances, but you kept your head and pulled through for her.''

"Thank you, sir. I appreciate it, but the truth is, I just did what anyone would have done. I'm hardly anybody's idea of a hero.''

"I doubt you'd get the new mama to agree to that.''

"Oh, she's just grateful, that's all.'' He noticed that the old man showed no inclination to be on his way. "Is there something else?''

"Well, you could do me a favor, if you have the time.''

"Now?'' Hardy asked, trying not to let his dismay show.

"Not right this second, but tonight. Like I said, only if you have the time. I know what a busy social life you have.''

Hardy searched for a hint of censure in his tone, but couldn't find any. "The truth is I thought I'd skip going into town tonight. It's been a long day.''

Harlan Adams beamed, clearly ignoring Hardy's hint that he was exhausted. "Terrific. Then you have some time on your hands.''

"I suppose. What can I do for you?''

"I'd like you to take a ride over to my son's and have a look at one of the horses.'' His expression turned regretful. "I declare, Jordan might have grown up on this ranch, but what he knows about animals wouldn't fill a thimble.''

"Wouldn't Slade be better for the job? He's the expert with horses.''

The old man was undeterred by his logic. "He's

tied up tonight or I'd have asked him. Since you're free, would you mind? Kelly's been real worried about a little filly she's got over there.''

Hardy sensed a trap, but for the life of him he couldn't figure out what it might be. ''Let me clean up, have supper, and I'll ride on over.''

''Take a shower, if you want, but forget supper. Kelly will have something for you over there. She's quite a cook. Better than Sweeney any day of the week. She said it's the least she can do to thank you for taking the trouble to stop by.''

Nothing about this added up. There were a dozen or more men around White Pines who were every bit as qualified to look at that horse as Hardy was, some more so. To top it off, Kelly and Jordan's daughter, Dani, was a vet. Granted, she dealt primarily with small animals, but she surely could have examined the horse if her mother was so worked up about it. Add in the offer of dinner and Hardy was all but convinced there was something odd going on. He just couldn't figure out what.

Well, it hardly mattered now. He was committed. He'd find out soon enough.

''If you speak to Kelly, tell her I'll be by in forty-five minutes or so,'' he advised Harlan Adams.

''Will do, son. Thanks. It will put her mind at ease, I'm sure.''

He turned and walked off, whistling something that sounded suspiciously upbeat. Harlan Patrick arrived just in time to see him go.

''What was Grandpa Harlan doing here?''

''Beats me,'' Hardy said. ''Something about a

sick horse at your uncle's. He wants me to take a look at it.''

''And you agreed?''

''Why not? I couldn't see how I could say no.''

To his astonishment, Harlan Patrick burst out laughing.

Hardy's gaze narrowed. ''Okay, what's going on? What do you know that I don't?''

His friend held up his hands and backed off. ''Oh, no, I'm not getting in the middle of this.''

''In the middle of what?''

''Nothing. Not a thing.'' He winked. ''You have yourself a fine evening, Hardy. Something tells me it's going to be downright fascinating. I might just drop on over to my uncle's myself. Haven't seen Jordan and Kelly in ages.''

Harlan Patrick's gleeful response nagged at Hardy the whole time he was showering and changing into something halfway presentable. When he was ready, he hopped into his pickup and made the short drive to the ranch that had belonged to Kelly's family for years. She had saved it singlehandedly after her folks died, and even though she and Jordan could have built something far more lavish on the property, they had kept the small, original house and simply added a few luxurious amenities to it. Hardy had been inside on a few occasions and admired the lack of pretension. This was a home, not a show-place.

When he pulled to a stop in front, he debated whether he should just go around to the corral, but finally decided on trying the front door first. As he stood on the porch waiting for someone to answer his knock, he thought he heard crying. Something about the sound reminded him of the wails of another baby, a baby he had held in his arms just the day before.

"Why that sneaky old coot," he muttered under his breath just as the door opened.

"Hardy, you're here," Kelly said just a shade too cheerfully. "I can't tell you how grateful I am that you had time to stop by tonight. Come on in."

He stayed right where he was, still stunned by the baby's cries. "Why don't I just go on around back and take a look at the horse. No need to go tromping through the house. Sounds as if you have enough commotion in there."

Kelly sighed. "I was afraid you'd hear that. Laura doesn't waste any time letting us know when she's ready for a meal."

"Laura," he echoed, his worst suspicions confirmed. "Trish's baby?"

Guilty patches of color flared in Kelly's cheeks. Then her chin went up a defiant notch. She might be an Adams by marriage, but she was as brazen as the rest of them. "Yes. They're staying with us for a bit."

"Funny, no one mentioned that to me."

The color in her cheeks faded, and she actually managed to look totally innocent as she said, "Really? It was hardly a secret."

"Just tell me one thing."

"What's that?"

"Do you really have a sick horse?"

"Well, of course I do," she declared with a touch of indignation. "Surely you don't think I'd lie about a thing like that."

"Lie? Maybe not. Shade the truth a little? Now that's a whole different kettle of fish. As for your father-in-law, it seems to me he might flat-out fib if it suited his purposes."

"Yes, Harlan does have a way of shaping the world around him to his own ends," she admitted. "The rest of us prefer subtlety."

She met his gaze directly, "Are you coming in? Or are you going to go away mad?"

He wanted very badly to turn around and stalk away in a huff, but listening to Laura bellowing had reminded him of just how many times he'd thought of her in the past 24 hours. As for her mama, she'd been on his mind a lot, too. What could it hurt to stop in and make sure the two of them were doing okay? A quick little visit didn't mean anything.

"I'll stay," he said finally. "Just long enough to say hello to Trish and take a look at that horse. No dinner, okay?"

"Whatever you say," she agreed with a beaming smile. "Whatever makes you comfortable. Can I get you something to drink? Some coffee maybe? It's downright frigid out there and I know you've been outside all day."

"Coffee would be fine."

Kelly nodded. "Go on in the living room and say hello, then. I'll bring that coffee right in." She gave him a little shove as if she weren't entirely certain that he'd go in on his own.

Hardy stood just outside the living room and watched as Trish tried to soothe the baby, whose howls were showing no signs of letting up. Trish's hair was a tangled mess, as if she'd been combing her fingers frantically through it. Her complexion was pale. He wondered just how long she'd been pacing with the irritable baby.

"Sweetie, I don't know what else to do," she whispered, her voice filled with frustration. She looked as if she might burst into tears. "You've had your dinner. Your diaper's been changed."

"Mind if I give it a try?" Hardy asked, taking pity on her. He wasn't much of an expert, but at least he could give Trish a break so she could get herself together before she fainted from pure exhaustion.

She shot a startled gaze in his direction. "Hardy! I had no idea you were here."

"Then we're even," he said dryly.

"What?"

"Never mind." He held out his arms. "Hand her over."

She hesitated for an instant, then placed Laura in his outstretched hands. "I can't imagine what's wrong with her."

He held the baby in front his face for an instant. "Hey, there, missy. What's all the fuss about?" he inquired. "You're giving your mama a tough time."

The cries died down. The baby's gaze wandered as if trying to search out the source of this unfamiliar voice.

"Better," he soothed. "But let's try to stop altogether, okay, sweet thing?"

He put the baby on his shoulder and rubbed her back. Before long, a huge belch filled the air. He grinned.

"Oh, my," Trish murmured. "That's all it was? She needed to be burped?"

"Could be."

Trish sank into a chair and stared at him miserably. "I'm lousy at this. What on earth ever made me think I could be a mother?"

"For starters, you're a female," Hardy reminded her. "Even though you got yourself into a pickle the other night out on that road, you strike me as being smart enough. You've only been at this a couple of days now. Give it a month. If mothering is still eluding you then, we'll talk again."

"What will you do? Take over?"

He chuckled. "You never know. I might have a knack for it."

"Look at her," Trish said. "She's sound asleep. I'd say you definitely have a knack for it. Come on, I'll take her and put her down."

"Oh, no you don't," Hardy said, reluctant to give up the baby. She felt right in his arms, as if she were something he'd been missing without even knowing it. "I did the hard work. Now I get the payoff."

She regarded him with amazement. "You want to hold her."

"Why not?"

"I don't know. I just figured you might want to get on with whatever you came here to do."

Hardy remembered the horse. He also remembered the coffee that Kelly had never brought. He had a hunch he was already doing exactly what he'd been lured here to do.

"How did you end up here, anyway?" he asked Trish.

"I think Lizzy had a hand in it. I'm pretty sure she talked to Kelly and Jordan. He and my father are business associates. I think they're pretty uncomfortable with the fact that I don't want my father to know I'm here, but they invited me to stay a while anyway. It'll just be for a few days."

He settled into a chair with the baby, then asked, "And then what?"

"I'll move on."

"To?"

"I'm not sure."

"But you won't be going home?"

"No, that's one thing I know for sure. I won't be going home."

"Why not?"

"If you knew my father, you wouldn't have to ask that. He's the ultimate control freak. Add in my mother, who is horrified by my decision to have the baby on my own, and it seems like home is the last place for me to be."

Hardy thought over what she'd said, then recalled something he'd heard on the news earlier about some Dallas bigwig's missing daughter. "Delacourt? Your father wouldn't be Bryce Delacourt, would he? The oilman?"

She returned his gaze ruefully. "Afraid so."

"Oh, boy."

She immediately looked alarmed. "What?"

"He's got the whole blasted country looking for you. This may be a tiny place, but you've made a big impression. It won't be long before word leaks out that you're here. Don't you think it would be better to call him, so he knows you're okay? He might call off his dogs then. It also might be easier on Kelly and Jordan. I suspect he won't like the fact that his friends kept your whereabouts from him."

"No, he won't," she admitted with a sigh. Then she regarded him intently. "But I can't tell him. You can't, either. Promise me, please."

"Look, darlin', I'm not in the habit of ratting out my friends, but not everybody's going to feel that way, especially if that reward he's offering gets much bigger."

Trish looked horrified. "He's offering a reward? As if I'm a common criminal or something?"

"More like he's a desperate father," he replied reasonably.

"Oh, no. You don't know Bryce Delacourt. This isn't about desperation. This is about him being ticked off because I slipped out and he can't find me. It's about him not being able to control me."

She took four agitated strides across the room and grabbed up the phone. She punched in the numbers with enough force to have the phone bouncing on the table.

"Miriam, it's me. Is my father around?" Her foot tapped impatiently as she waited. Her eyes flashed sparks of pure fury.

Even from halfway across the room, Hardy could hear a man he assumed to be her father bellowing out a string of questions. Trish waited until he fell silent.

"Are you through?" she asked quietly. "Good. Because I am only going to say this once. Call off the detectives. Tell the media that I've been found and that I am perfectly fine, that it was all a huge misunderstanding and that you're terribly sorry for having sent everyone on such a wild-goose chase."

She listened for a moment, then shook her head. "No, I am not coming home. No, I am not going to tell you where I am. I am fine. So is your grand-daughter, in case you're interested. We're both do-ing just great. If you ever hope to see either of us again, you will give me some space now. Are we clear?"

Whatever her father said to that was too softly spoken for Hardy to hear, but her expression soft-ened finally. She sighed.

"Yes, Daddy, I love you, too," she whispered. "I'll be in touch. I promise."

When she turned around, there were tears stream-ing down her cheeks. Hardy stood up, put the baby into the nearby carrier, then went to her. He touched a finger to her cheek, brushed away the dampness.

"You okay?"

She managed a watery smile. "Better now," she said.

"Remind me not to tick you off."

She gave him a full-fledged grin. "Oh, that.

Sometimes yelling is the only way to get through to him. Delacourts tend to be stubborn.''

He laughed. ''Yeah, I got that part.''

''Thank you for warning me about what was going on, so I could stop him from turning Los Piños into a circus.''

''Do you honestly think he'll give up the search?''

''If he wants to see his granddaughter he will. And he knows I meant that, too. He may be difficult, but he's not stupid. Now that he's certain I'm okay, he'll give me some space.''

''For how long?''

''Until he thinks it's time to come charging after me,'' she admitted. ''I figure I've got a month tops to find a place to settle down and get my new life on track. I have to have every little piece in place or he'll run roughshod over me until he gets his way.''

''What exactly does he want?''

''He wants me to come home and marry Laura's father.''

Hardy was surprised by just how deeply he detested that idea himself. ''And you disagree?''

''Oh, yes,'' she said fervently. ''It won't happen. Not now. Not ever.''

Because relief flooded through him at her response, Hardy knew it was time to go.

''You going to be okay?'' he asked, grabbing his jacket off a chair.

''Sure.''

He nodded. ''Keep your chin up, darlin'. Something tells me everything is going to work out just the way you want it to.''

''Do you carry a crystal ball around in your pocket?''

''Nope, but anybody hearing you stand up for yourself just now would put their money on you.''

She seemed startled by the comment, but a smile began tugging at her lips. ''Thanks, I think.''

''Oh, it was a compliment, sweetheart. Make no mistake about that.'' He winked at her. ''Tell Kelly if she checks, I suspect that horse of hers is just fine now.''

Trish stared at him blankly. ''What horse?''

''Just tell her. She'll understand.''

He took off then, before the yearning to stay became so powerful that he forgot all the million and one reasons he had for getting out before he landed squarely in the middle of emotional quicksand.

Chapter Five

Hardy had actually paid her a compliment, Trish thought, staring after him with what was probably a ridiculously silly grin. She'd finally been exposed to a sampling of that famed charm of his, albeit little more than a couple of softly spoken endearments. She could see how it might be totally devastating if fully unleashed.

There were the dimples, for one thing. For another, his eyes shot off sparks like a live wire, turning the amber color to something closer to an unusual glittering bronze. And there were the occasional glimpses of his wit. She could see how the combination could be wickedly seductive.

Of course, she was immune to all of it. She'd been down that path all too recently. She'd sworn off men with good looks and glib tongues. Since that was the case, why did she feel as if she'd finally passed some sort of a test?

She was still standing where he'd left her when Kelly walked in, a cup of coffee in hand.

"Where's Hardy?" she asked.

She glanced around as if expecting to find him still lurking in the shadows. Her behavior might have been more believable if her timing hadn't been so obvious. She'd shooed him into the room nearly an hour before, promising coffee as she'd breezed off into the kitchen. Even if she'd had to grind the beans and brew enough for an army, it would have been ready before now. She'd deliberately waited to give Trish plenty of time alone with him.

"He had to go," Trish explained, playing along with whatever game her hostess was up to. "He said to tell you he thought the horse was fine."

Kelly looked vaguely guilty. "Great. Did he go out to check her?"

"Actually, no. I thought that was a little odd myself." She peered intently at Kelly. "Any idea what he meant?"

"Just a mix-up," Kelly said blithely. "Crossed signals. You know, one of those things."

Trish's gaze narrowed. She might not know Kelly all that well, but she recognized a schemer when she saw one. She'd lived with the type most of her life. She'd been warned about Harlan Adams. She'd even guessed that Lizzy came from the same matchmaking gene pool. Now it appeared she was going to have to stay on her toes around Kelly Adams, too.

"One of what things?" she inquired in a silky tone that belied her agitation. "Something tells me you'd better explain."

Kelly patted her hand. "Never mind. It's not important. Did you two have a good visit?"

"After he managed to do what I couldn't, calm Laura down," she conceded. "Apparently his skills with the ladies even extends to those only a couple of days old."

"That's Hardy, all right. The kids around here tend to gravitate toward him. He's extraordinarily patient with them," she enthused. "Underneath that devil-may-care attitude, he's a good, solid man."

Trish smiled at her. "You don't have to sell him to me. He saved my life, more than likely, and brought Laura safely into the world. I'll always be in his debt." Her expression sobered. "But that's all."

"Oh, of course," Kelly said hurriedly, but without real conviction. "You just met. What more could there be?"

"Exactly."

"So," she began with obviously undeterred fascination, "what else did you two talk about?"

Trish sighed as she recalled the primary topic of conversation. "He told me my father's reported me missing."

Kelly's eyes widened. "Oh, dear. I hadn't heard that."

"Hardy said he heard it on the news. Don't worry. I called my father and warned him to call off the bloodhounds. I'm pretty sure he will."

"Did you tell him where you were?"

"And have him come charging over here tonight? Not a chance."

"Trish…"

"Don't even try. It has to be this way, at least for now. If that's going to be a problem for you or Jordan, I can move on," she said, reiterating her earlier offer to go, rather than involve them in a sticky situation. "I don't want to put you in the middle of my battle."

"Believe me, we're used to being caught up in squabbles around here. We can take it," Kelly reassured her. "But we also believe, in the end, that family counts more than anything."

"I know. I doubt there's anyone in Texas who doesn't know just how tight-knit the Adamses are. My brothers and I are extremely close, too. I'd contact them if it wouldn't just put them in the position of having to lie to our parents. I'm not going to get into everything, but I will say that the senior Delacourts are cut from very different cloth."

Kelly regarded her somberly. "If that's true, then it's a pity."

"Oh, it's true enough."

"Then for the time being, just think of us as family. We'll be right here for you until you're completely back on your feet again."

"Thank you," Trish said. "I can't tell you how much that means to me."

"It's our privilege to have you here," Kelly assured her with absolute sincerity, then grinned. "It doesn't mean I'll stop nagging you about opening the lines of communication with your own family, though.''

Trish laughed at the openly declared warning. ''Fair enough.''

When Kelly had gone off to finish getting dinner ready, Trish settled back against the chair's soft cushions and let her eyes drift shut. She had to think about the future, had to plan her next move, but just for now she felt more at home and at ease than she had in months.

''So, how was dinner last night?'' Harlan Patrick asked when Hardy joined him to ride out in the morning.

''I picked up a couple of burgers in town,'' Hardy replied, keeping his gaze averted. He could just imagine the shocked expression on his friend's face.

''I thought you were going to eat over at Kelly's,'' he said, clearly puzzled.

''Plans changed,'' Hardy said succinctly.

''Why is that?''

''It seems the whole thing was a bit of a mix-up. The horse was fine. I took off. End of subject.'' He climbed into the saddle and spurred his horse to a canter.

Harlan Patrick scrambled to catch up. ''What about...?'' His voice trailed off.

Hardy turned and regarded him with exaggerated curiosity. ''What about what?''

Harlan Patrick scowled. ''You know perfectly well what I'm asking about.''

''Do I?''

"Trish and the baby, blast it. Did you see them?"

"Hard to miss them. Little Laura was howling like a banshee when I got there. Funny how nobody thought to mention before I went over there that she and her mama were staying at your uncle's."

"I figured you knew," Harlan Patrick said defensively, then grinned. "Seeing how tight you two are."

"We are not tight," Hardy said. "I barely even know the woman."

He just knew that her skin was soft, that her eyes flooded with tears at the drop of a hat, that she smelled like something exotic and spicy. He also knew that she rattled him more than any woman he'd ever met. Under the circumstances, those were more than enough reasons to give her a wide berth.

"Any plans to see her again?" Harlan Patrick inquired innocently.

"Not on your life."

Harlan Patrick chuckled at the fierce response. "Oh, really?" he said doubtfully. "I've never known you to protest so loudly about spending time with a beautiful woman."

"A beautiful woman with a brand-new baby," Hardy reminded him. "I'm not in the market for a ready-made family. I'm the love 'em and leave 'em type, remember?"

"Funny thing about types," Harlan Patrick mused. "Love comes along, and things change faster than lightning."

Hardy scowled at him. "You don't know what you're talking about. You were a lousy bachelor.

You never had eyes for anyone except Laurie. Even when she dumped you, it was like pulling teeth to get you to go out with another woman.''

''True enough, but I've seen enough confirmed bachelors bite the dust to know that all it takes is the right woman, the right timing and a little nudge.''

''Well, you can keep any ideas you have about nudging to yourself,'' Hardy declared, then added, ''You might pass that along to anyone else who might be getting ideas, including your grandfather. Last night had to be his sneaky idea, though your aunt Kelly was clearly in on it, too. I'd hate to have to flee to Montana just to get away from all the scheming that goes on around here.''

Harlan Patrick shook his head. ''Oh, brother, are you in trouble. Any time a man has to skip town just to steer clear of a woman he claims to have absolutely no interest in, he's in so deep, it'd take a tow truck to extricate him.''

Hardy faced him squarely. ''I am not interested in Trish Delacourt. I am not interested in a serious, long-term relationship with any woman. I don't know how I can say it any plainer than that.''

He rode off, leaving Harlan Patrick howling with laughter. The sound followed him, setting his nerves on edge and stiffening his resolve. No one was going to trap him into marriage. No one was going to turn him into a daddy for a kid who wasn't his own. No one was going to…

An image of Trish flashed in his head, as if to stubbornly remind him that he might be able to control his actions, but not his thoughts. Obviously, she was going to plague him whether he liked it or not.

''Terrific,'' he muttered, digging his spurs into his horse until they were flying and all he could think about was staying in the saddle.

That night when his temper had cooled and his nerves had calmed, he concluded that what he desperately needed was a hot date, someone who could get his mind off of a smart-mouthed, blond beauty with vulnerable eyes.

He dug out his little black book, settled beside the phone in the bunkhouse and began leafing through pages. Normally the process didn't take more than a minute. He could decide on which female suited his mood faster than most men selected a steak from the menu.

Not tonight, though. He seemed stuck on finding faults. Fran's laugh was a little too loud. Paula hadn't had a real thought in all of her twenty-five years. Renata painted her fingernails blue, for Pete's sake. Ursula—now there was a beauty, he thought appreciatively—unfortunately chattered incessantly. Mindy annoyingly hung on his every word. Jan argued over everything.

He sighed heavily and snapped the book shut. Funny how none of those traits had ever bothered him before. Maybe what he needed was a new woman. Of course, single females he didn't already know were in short supply in Los Piños. The selection wasn't much better if he expanded the search to Garden City. Flying to Dallas just to find a date that would banish thoughts of Trish Delacourt from his head seemed a little extreme. Some might view it as a sign that he was in over his head with the pretty new mama in town.

Finally he settled for taking a drive back to the End of the Road Saloon in Garden City, the last place he'd spent a peaceful, albeit lonely, evening. Maybe Rita would be around and would have another indecent suggestion that would get his juices flowing.

Of course, on the way he would have to drive past Jordan and Kelly's without giving in to the sudden temptation to stop by and check on Trish and Laura. He might have made it, too, if he hadn't spotted Trish, all bundled up for the cold weather, at the end of the lane looking as if she were about to collapse. She was clinging to the gate just to stay upright. He swerved into the driveway and leaped from the truck.

"What are you doing out here?" he demanded irritably. "Trying to get yourself killed the other night wasn't enough? You had to try it again."

"I just went for a walk," she said. "I'll catch my breath and be fine in a minute. Then I'll walk back. No need to trouble yourself on my behalf."

"You will not walk back," he argued. "Get in the truck."

"I will not get in the truck," she said, that stubborn little chin of hers shooting into the air.

Hardy scowled at her. "Would you rather collapse out here than accept a ride back with me?"

"Yes," she insisted.

He regarded her with bemusement. "Why?"

"Because it is too humiliating. Because you will throw it in my face. Shall I go on?"

"Try a reason that makes sense," he suggested, swallowing the urge to smile. She was clearly in no mood to discover that she was providing him with the best entertainment he'd had all day.

"Okay," he said at last. "We'll compromise. Are you familiar with the concept?"

She frowned at his teasing.

He nodded as if she'd actually responded. "Good. Then here's the plan. I will walk back to the house with you. That way if you collapse en route, I will be there to catch you. Deal?"

"It will still be humiliating," she grumbled. "You will still throw it in my face."

"Probably," he agreed. "But it's the best deal you're going to get. I walk with you or I toss you over my shoulder and put you in the truck. What's it going to be?"

She set off on foot without bothering to respond. Hardy couldn't control the laughter that bubbled up this time. Her scowl deepened and she kept her gaze averted as she plodded along. He had a tough time slowing his pace to her hobbling gait. He had to control the urge to save her from her stubborn pride and toss her over his shoulder. He figured she might protest that so loudly that half the Adamses would come flying. The resulting explanations would only complicate his life. He could just imagine the twist Kelly and the others would put on his concern.

They walked in silence for a hundred yards or so

before he asked, "Have you always had such an independent streak?"

"Always."

"Get you in much trouble?"

She finally slid a glance his way and grinned. "More than you can imagine. The other night pretty much tops the list, though. I guess you've been unlucky enough to catch me at my worst."

If this was her worst, he had a feeling he was extremely fortunate not to have been around to sample her best. He would probably have found her irresistible. As it was, he found her pluck annoying and ill-advised, but admirable just the same. And that was without adding in the hormonal punch she packed.

"What exactly do you do when you're not running away from home, having babies by the side of the road and taking a hike when you should be in bed?" he asked. He had a feeling she could command a small army, if she was of a mind to.

"Nothing right now," she admitted. "I sold my business before I left Houston."

"What sort of business?"

"A dinosaur, really. A small, independent bookstore. I specialized in mysteries mostly, which gave me a niche and a loyal customer base. I even had a mail-order catalogue and Internet Web page that were doing really well."

"I thought all the independent bookstores were being forced into bankruptcy by the big chains," he said. "That Meg Ryan movie that made a fortune a while back was about that."

"Which is why everyone told me I was nuts," she agreed. "But with good customer service, the right niche, the right location and some innovative marketing, it's possible to survive."

"Why not do that here?" he asked. He almost groaned aloud the instant the words were out of his mouth. Was he nuts? He'd spoken before he considered the implication. As soon as he'd said it, he regretted the suggestion. Hadn't he just lectured himself about the dangers of doing anything at all to keep Trish around town? He was usually a whole lot more careful about the words he uttered around any female.

She stopped so fast, he almost charged right into her. "Here?" she echoed as if he'd suggested setting up shop on Mars.

"Probably not a good idea," he said hurriedly. "It's a small town. You'd go broke in a month."

As if she hadn't even heard him, her expression turned thoughtful. She began to move again, albeit at an even slower pace. "There's no bookstore in town?"

He sighed, then reluctantly admitted what she could discover in ten seconds on her own anyway. "No."

"What about Garden City?"

"I think there's one at the mall, but no superstore, if that's what you're asking."

"Hmm."

He could practically see the wheels turning as she toyed with the idea. As for him, his palms started turning sweaty, and his stomach began churning as he realized she'd taken him seriously and was actually considering settling down in Los Piños. Heaven help him!

"Property downtown probably has very low overhead," she mused. "I could create a new catalogue and a jazzy new Web page. Legally I'd probably have to expand beyond mysteries and be a full-service bookstore, so I wouldn't be competing directly with the business I sold. Maybe I could add in a lot of Westerns. That might do really well on a Web page. I've heard stores in other parts of the country don't stock that many beyond Louis L'Amour and Zane Grey." She gazed at him with sparkling eyes. "What do you think?"

"It sounds like a possibility," he said neutrally, regretting his lack of nerve to tell her it was insane so she'd forget all about it.

"Maybe I'll drive into town tomorrow and take a look at what's available."

"You shouldn't be driving," he scolded, seizing on any excuse he could think of to delay her putting this impetuous plan into action. Maybe if he could stall her long enough, she'd forget all about it.

"Thank you, Dr. Jones," she retorted.

He snatched another excuse out of thin air. "Besides, your car's still in a ditch."

"No, it isn't. Jordan arranged to have it towed, checked out and brought over here this morning."

"You still shouldn't be driving," Hardy insisted. "Surely that's just good common sense. After all, you just had a baby."

"In some parts of the world, women have babies

out in the field and get right back to work,'' she pointed out.

Having just seen firsthand how difficult giving birth was, Hardy shuddered. "It can't be good for them."

"I'm not saying it is. I'm just saying that giving birth is natural. It doesn't turn you into an invalid."

"Whatever you say. If you're getting a little stir-crazy sitting around, I'm sure Kelly can find some chores for you to do. Scrubbing floors and washing windows, maybe. Or maybe you'd like to ride out and round up some cattle with me?"

He'd been teasing, but her expression immediately brightened. "Oh, could I? I've always wanted to do that."

He stared at her incredulously. "You actually want to bounce around in a saddle?"

She winced. "Well, maybe not today, but soon. You won't forget, will you?"

Hardy had a hunch she wouldn't allow him to. Since she didn't seem to have a lick of common sense, he said, "Look, if you can wait till tomorrow evening to go into town, I'll take you. We can grab some dinner and then cruise up and down Main Street to see if any property is available. I doubt there's much. Most of the businesses have been there since the town was first settled."

"Then it's time a new one came along to shake things up," she said, undaunted by his deliberately discouraging assessment.

They had reached the porch. Hardy stood at the foot of the steps, determined not to set foot inside that house where all manner of schemers lurked. Where Laura might be around needing to be held, he conceded; that was the real threat.

"The baby's doing okay?" he inquired, forcing himself to act as if the question were no more than idle curiosity.

"She's fine," Trish said, beaming. "The best thing I've ever done. Want to come in and see her?"

"Not tonight," he said a little too hurriedly.

She gave him an oddly knowing look, then shrugged. "Whatever. I'll see you tomorrow then. What time?"

"Six o'clock okay?"

"Perfect. I can get Laura fed and she'll stay down for a few hours. I'll make sure it's okay with Kelly if I leave her here."

"Oh, I doubt she'll object," Hardy said dryly. In fact, if he had to put money on it, he'd bet that Kelly would do a little jig in the street when she discovered that Trish was thinking of staying and that it had been his idea.

Obviously, he'd lost his mind.

Chapter Six

Maybe he could still talk her out of staying in Los Piños, Hardy consoled himself as he drove over to pick up Trish the next night. After all, the decision hadn't been carved in granite.

He had told absolutely no one about his impulsive, ill-considered idea. He just prayed that it would come to nothing and no one would ever find out about it. He was taking enough ribbing about Trish and the baby as it was. If people found out he'd all but asked her to stick around town, they would make way too much of it.

"Come on in," Kelly said, greeting him at the door with a beaming smile.

Hardy took one look at her expression and concluded he was already out of luck. She knew. Either

Trish had already blabbed about the reason for this excursion or Kelly had drawn her own conclusions. Either way, his goose was cooked.

"I can wait out here," he said, hoping to forestall a cross-examination. "Unless it's going to be a while."

"No, she'll be right down. She's just checking on the baby one last time." She gave him a knowing look. "You aren't afraid I'm going to subject you to some sort of inquisition if you come inside, are you?"

"Of course not," he lied.

"Well then, I don't see any need for the two of us to stand out here freezing. Jordan's away on business, so you're safe on that front, too."

He forced a smile. "Not to be disrespectful, but you really are a handful, aren't you?"

She grinned. "I certainly try to be. It keeps marriage from getting stale."

Hardy stepped inside, then stood there, warily eyeing Kelly Adams. She was all but popping with curiosity. He figured her promise not to subject him to a string of nosy questions was likely to be as short-lived as his resolve to steer clear of Trish. She didn't disappoint him.

"I hear you suggested Trish open a bookstore right here in Los Piños," she said conversationally.

"It didn't happen exactly like that, but yes, I suppose I'm the one who planted the idea."

"I think it's a brilliant idea. It would be wonderful not to have to drive all the way over to Garden City just to pick up a paperback."

"Sharon Lynn stocks paperbacks at Dolan's," he pointed out. "Maybe she's thinking of expanding. How's she going to feel about a bookstore going in?"

"She only carries a few bestsellers," Kelly said dismissively. "Not nearly enough for an avid reader. Besides, she thinks they're a nuisance."

He twisted his hat in his hands. "Yeah, well, it probably won't work out. I doubt there's any property available on Main Street."

"Actually, there is," Kelly said, clearly enjoying his discomfort. "I checked it out today. That little tailor shop right next door to Dolan's is closing. I think it's the perfect size for a bookstore, don't you? With a little work, it would be wonderfully cozy. And the rent is reasonable. More than reasonable, really. Trish couldn't believe it."

Hardy bit back a groan. "Harlan Adams wouldn't by any chance own that property, would he?" he asked suspiciously. If the man hadn't owned it this morning, he probably did by now.

Kelly beamed. "Why, as a matter of fact, he does."

"I don't suppose it was his idea to boot the tailor shop out of there?"

"Of course not. Willetta's eyes aren't what they used to be. Can't thread a needle if you can't see, you know. She's been wanting to retire for a long time. She finally made the decision to join her sister in Arizona."

It wouldn't surprise Hardy to discover that Harlan

Adams was paying her moving expenses and giving her some sort of payoff to get her out of there.

"Funny, I hadn't heard a thing about that," he said, watching Kelly's face for any sign of a telltale blush. She didn't so much as blink.

"It was a recent decision," she told him, then glanced upstairs. "Oh, here's Trish now. Doesn't she look wonderful?"

Hardy didn't need any coaching to agree. She looked fabulous. She was wearing a dark-blue wool skirt that fell to midcalf, boots, and a pale-blue sweater that looked so soft he had to stop himself from reaching out to brush his fingers over it. She'd worn her hair down, so that it skimmed her shoulders in soft waves. Suddenly he felt just as he had in high school when he'd picked up his date for the senior prom. He was flustered and tongue-tied. Why was it this woman could reduce him to a jumble of nerves, when no other woman on earth could?

"Ready to go?" he asked, his tone brusque.

"Absolutely."

He turned to Kelly. "We won't be long," he said, as if she'd just reminded him of some curfew.

"Stay as long as you like," she retorted, her eyes glittering with amusement. "I don't have any plans for this evening. Laura and I will be just fine."

After they were settled in his truck and on the way, Trish turned in the seat to face him. "It's very nice of you to do this," she said.

"No problem."

"It's great to be able to start thinking about the future, making plans. For a long time all I thought about was getting away from Houston, away from my father, away from…well, everything.''

"Including Laura's father?"

"Him most of all, I suppose."

"Have you told him about her?"

"No, but I'm sure my father has. They're very tight."

Hardy gritted his teeth. "Is that so?"

"Jack works for him. He's been envisioning a vice presidency ever since he and I started dating. I'm sure it must be a huge disappointment to him to think he might actually have to earn it."

Hardy shot a look at her. "You don't think much of the man, do you?"

"I did for a while. He was handsome and charming. He courted me with fancy dinners and thoughtful little gifts. I got caught up in the romance."

"Doesn't sound so bad to me. What happened?"

"It turned out I was only one of the women being treated to such attention." She made a face. "I've never been fond of being part of a crowd, especially when I'm the one wearing an engagement ring. I made a rather public scene and broke it off the same day I found out I was pregnant."

"Lousy timing," he observed.

"I don't suppose there's any good time to make a discovery like that, but in a way I'm glad it happened when it did. What if I'd actually married the jerk and then found out? Bottom line, Laura and I are both better off without him."

"But your folks don't see it that way?"

"Oh, no. They had visions of us being one big

happy family. Still do. The more distance I keep between us until they accept my decision, the better. My father tends to bulldoze over any decision he finds inconvenient. He found my decision to dump Jack extremely inconvenient. It's left him with a gap in his executive staff. He can't very well make Jack a vice president when all of Houston society knows what happened between him and me. The whole country club witnessed me dropping my engagement ring down the overexposed cleavage of one of his girlfriends.''

Hardy laughed, which earned him a scowl.

''It wasn't funny,'' she chided.

''I'm sure it wasn't at the time, but you have to admit it made quite a statement. I'm impressed.''

Her lips twitched ever so slightly. ''Yes, I suppose it did. I always wondered, though, which of them retrieved it. Jack, probably. The diamond was worth a fortune, and she didn't strike me as a keeper.''

''So you packed up and took off?''

''Not right away. I had to plan for it. I had to sell my business, close up my apartment and do it all without my father getting suspicious. He would have locked me in my room at the family mansion if he'd guessed what my intentions were.''

''Being cut off from your family must be difficult. Obviously he loves you or he wouldn't have stirred up such a ruckus when he realized you were missing.''

She shrugged. ''He does love me, in his way. So does my mother. But they're both more concerned about how what I do reflects on them than whether or not I'm happy. They hated my bookstore. It wasn't in the right neighborhood. It didn't cater to the right clientele. My father referred to it as my little hobby. It drove him crazy that it operated in the black and I didn't have to keep running to him for money to prop it up. He'd be shocked to find out what I got for it when I sold it.''

Hardy saw an opportunity to slow down her rush to open a bookstore in Los Piños. "Then you don't have to go back to work right away? You could stay home with Laura for a while?''

"Not immediately, no, but I can't live off the money forever. I have to use it to start over.''

They finally hit the outskirts of town and her gaze was promptly drawn to the main street of Los Piños. Hardy tried to see it through her eyes. Compared to the high-rise splendor of Houston, it must seem like a shabby distant cousin. Not that the storefronts were dilapidated. In fact, most of them had been spruced up, but they were small, family-owned restaurants and practical businesses designed for the local residents. There wasn't an expensive boutique or a fancy café among them.

"Oh, it's charming,'' she declared, her eyes shining. "I feel as if I've stepped into the middle of *Our Town.* It's like something from another era. Which shop is the one Kelly said is available? She said it was next to someplace called Dolan's.''

Hardy pointed out the drugstore. "Dolan's is owned by Kelly's niece, Sharon Lynn. Her mother used to run the lunch counter inside and then Sharon

Lynn followed in her footsteps. When old man Dolan decided to retire, Sharon Lynn bought him out. She's modernized it some, but it's still basically the same way it's been since back in the thirties, a real old-fashioned drugstore and soda fountain.''

''And there's the tailor shop,'' Trish said, studying it intently. ''Can we park here? I'd like a closer look. I see a light inside. Maybe we can get in so I can look around.''

Hardy had a feeling Willetta was counting on it. She'd probably been asked to linger after hours in anticipation of just such an impromptu visit. Resigned, he pulled into a parking space out front. Trish was out of the car before he could turn off the engine.

''Are you coming?'' she called back impatiently.

''I didn't realize it was urgent,'' he muttered.

''I heard that.'' She grabbed his hand and tugged him toward the door. ''Shall I try it or knock?'' she wondered aloud, then settled the matter, by doing both simultaneously. ''Hello. Is anyone here?''

Willetta came in from the back, reading glasses perched on the end of her nose. She gave Hardy a sour look. ''Oh, it's you.''

''Hey, Willetta,'' he said, ignoring her brusque manner. He'd brought his mending by a time or two and they'd always gotten along well enough. She was just naturally cranky.

She turned to Trish and looked her up and down. Apparently the survey didn't satisfy her curiosity. ''Who are you?'' she demanded. ''I don't recall seeing you around town before.''

"Willetta, this is Trish Delacourt," Hardy explained. "She's interested in renting this space."

"Somebody told me about that," she said distractedly, moving to a desk and searching through the pile of papers scattered over it. "I wrote it down." She finally picked up a scrap of yellow paper. "Here it is. Trish Delacourt. Yes, that's what it says, all right."

Trish appeared startled. "Who told you I might be by?"

"Harlan, who else? The old coot's anxious to get a new tenant in here before the last one's even out the door. For all of his money, he's still a greedy old man."

"Harlan?" Trish echoed. "Harlan Adams?"

"Isn't that what I said? Are you deaf, girl?"

"No, I'm just surprised, that's all. I had no idea he was even involved."

"Owns the place," Hardy informed her, enjoying her startled reaction.

"I see."

"I doubt it," Hardy said grimly.

"Well, are you going to look around or waste time gabbing?" Willetta demanded. "I don't have all night. I've got to get home and get my dinner or I'll be up all night with indigestion."

Clearly taken aback by her abrupt demeanor, Trish hesitated. Hardy could have encouraged a quick departure right then, but he figured she'd only insist on coming back at a more convenient time. He tucked a hand under Trish's elbow.

"We'll look around," he told Willetta. "Won't take but a minute."

"Yes, thank you," Trish said. "I really appreciate you letting us interrupt your evening."

As near as Hardy could tell, there wasn't much to see. The tailor shop was one long, narrow room with a fireplace on one wall that looked as if it might still work, though it was doubtful it had been used in years. Halfway back, Willetta had hung a drape across a rod to close off a room where she kept material, took measurements and did her sewing. In front a few old mannequins displayed out-of-date dresses she had apparently designed. He tried to envision it with the clutter gone, the fireplace blazing and books lining the walls. His imagination didn't stretch that far.

Apparently, however, Trish's did. Her eyes were alight with excitement as she spun in a slow circle. "It's wonderful," she declared. "Could I see in the back?"

"Don't see why not," Willetta said. "Everybody else in town traipses back there."

Hardy followed as Trish opened the curtain and stepped into the back room. Only then did he realize just how deep the shop was. There was at least twice as much room in the back as in the front, plenty of room for a small bookstore.

"There's a storeroom that goes with it," Willetta grudgingly told them. "Runs behind the office next door." She pointed to a door. "Through there. There's a bathroom, too."

Trish eagerly opened the door and wandered

through. "Oh, my, it's huge," she announced. "More than enough room for stock and the mail-order operation." She turned her gaze on him. "It's perfect. And I can't believe the rent. Compared to Houston, it's a steal."

Hardy could see that the whole plan was spinning wildly out of his control. She was going to land smack in the middle of his life, and there was almost nothing he could see to do about it.

"You're in the middle of nowhere," he reminded her, trying to keep a desperate note out of his voice. "That's why it's so cheap."

"Internet. Mail order," she countered. "For those, location doesn't matter."

Giving up, he shrugged. "If you say so."

She spun around, then grabbed Willetta and hugged her, to the old woman's obvious astonishment. "Thank you. It's wonderful."

Willetta gathered her composure, then actually smiled. Hardy was surprised her face didn't crack under the strain.

"It's been a long time since I've seen that kind of optimism. Hope you don't live to regret this."

"I won't," Trish declared firmly. "When were you planning on closing your shop?"

"Eager to run me off, are you?"

"Absolutely not," Trish said, looking horrified. "I'm just trying to predict my own timetable."

"End of next week," Willetta said. "Will that suit you?"

"If you're sure it's not rushing you too much."

"Tell you the truth I'll be glad to get to Arizona,"

Willetta admitted. "I've just been hanging around here out of habit."

The two women actually beamed at each other. It had turned into a blasted lovefest. Hardy had to swallow back panic.

"We'd better be going so Willetta can get home," he said, interrupting Trish's chatter.

"Oh, of course," she apologized. "Unless you'd like to join us for dinner."

Willetta looked tempted for an instant, which would have suited Hardy just fine. She could have served as a buffer between him and Trish. For the last half hour, watching excitement put color in her cheeks and sparks in her eyes, he'd wanted desperately to kiss her. He figured it was going to take a natural disaster or the intercession of someone like Willetta to keep him from following through on the inclination before the night was over.

Instead, though, the seamstress patted Trish's hand. "No, indeed. I wouldn't dream of barging in on your date with your young man." She tugged Trish aside. "Keep your eye on him, though. I've heard stories."

Trish glanced his way. "Is that so?"

"Okay, that's enough," Hardy said. "Willetta, you're just jealous because I've never asked you out. You've forgotten all about the ice cream sundae I bought you at Dolan's last summer."

"Indeed, I haven't. It was butterscotch, as I recall."

He grinned. "That it was. Now don't you go telling tales about me to Trish."

"Young man, it will take more than one butter-scotch sundae to buy my silence."

He winked at her. "I'll tell Sharon Lynn to make you a banana split tomorrow, on me."

Willetta grinned. "Now you're talking," she enthused. "Now go on, you two. Get out of here."

When they were outside, Hardy suggested walking up the street to the Italian restaurant. "You'll need the walk after you eat. They serve enough to feed an army."

"Perfect. I'm starving." She glanced up at him. "You really are a shameless womanizer, aren't you?"

"Me?"

"Willetta's not the first person to suggest it."

"You shouldn't listen to gossip."

"Is it all lies?" she persisted.

Uncomfortable with the fact that the better part of it was actually pure fact, Hardy tried to think of an evasion. Then he recalled what had happened with her ex-fiancé. Maybe this was the answer. Maybe if she lumped him in with Jack the jerk, she'd keep him at arm's length. That would take the decision out of his hands. It was the perfect solution to the attraction that was beginning to drive him just a little crazy. He was beginning to think he wouldn't even make it through this evening without succumbing to temptation.

But for some reason, he didn't want Trish to think of him that way. It was important that she not classify him as a jerk.

"You're avoiding the question," she pointed out when his silence dragged on.

"I date a lot," he conceded finally. "But I'm not like your ex-fiancé. I don't have long-term relationships, and I don't cheat. I just enjoy playing the field."

"An interesting distinction."

"Look, I think what he did to you was lousy. He'd made a commitment. He should have honored it."

"So you think it's okay to play the field, as you put it, as long as everything's out in the open."

"Exactly. That way nobody has any illusions and nobody gets hurt."

"Bull," she declared.

He stopped and stared at her, shocked by her curt dismissal of his philosophy. "What?"

"You heard me. That's just a cop-out and you know it. I suppose you end every date by promising to call, because it's expected, and then never bothering to do it."

"I never do that," he retorted indignantly. "I never make promises of any kind that I don't intend to keep. Never."

"If you say so."

Hardy didn't like the disdain he heard in her voice. "Just how am I supposed to prove to you that I'm telling the truth?"

"Why should it matter to me one way or the other?"

"Maybe it doesn't, but it matters to me."

"Why?"

"Because…" His words faltered. "Just because."

"Just because you can't bear to have one single woman think you're anything other than a sexy, charming hunk?"

"No, of course not," he said, jerking open the door of the restaurant and standing back to allow her to precede him. The entire conversation was ruining his appetite. Not even the aroma of garlic and spices was enough to overcome the sudden churning of his stomach.

"Come on, admit it, Hardy. You like being the playboy of this part of the western world."

"I never said I didn't like that," he grumbled.

"You just don't want to be labeled as a bad guy."

"Right."

"Well, I say if the shoe fits…" She allowed her words to trail off as she sashayed on ahead and settled into a booth.

Hardy followed and slid in across from her. "You're a very annoying woman."

"So I've been told." She grinned at him. "And I am way out of your league."

He blinked and stared. "Excuse me? When did this turn personal? Have you heard me ask you out on a date?"

She peered at him over the top of the menu that had been handed to her by an overtly curious waitress. "What do you call this?"

"I brought you into town to look at property. That's it. End of story. I'm doing you a favor," he said. "This is definitely not a date."

"Feels like one to me," she said. "But, of course, you're the expert."

The waitress tried unsuccessfully to choke back a laugh. At Hardy's fierce look, she swallowed hard and asked, "Can I get you two something to drink? Maybe cool things off?"

"I'll have a beer," Hardy said. "What about you, Trish?"

"Herb tea, if you have it."

"Sorry," the waitress apologized.

"Anything nonalcoholic or decaf?"

"Orange soda."

Trish nodded. "Fine. I'll have that."

When the waitress had gone off to fetch their drinks—and probably tell everyone in the place about the very provocative conversation she'd overheard—Hardy stared hard at Trish. "Back to our discussion. You can ask any woman I've ever been out with if I misled her in any way. There's not a one who can say I did."

"That doesn't mean you didn't stir up hopes and then leave them unfulfilled," she said. She made it sound like an accusation of attempted armed robbery or worse.

"Darlin', I made it my business to fulfill their every little desire."

She made a face. "I am not talking about sex."

"Well, I am."

"Of course you are."

Hardy hadn't been struck by so many verbal blows in such a short period of time in all his years of going out with women. Of course, that was probably because he avoided the smart-mouthed variety like Trish as if they carried the plague. He had to concede, though, that the exchange was invigorating. It was also stirring up a whole lot of fascinating images of how explosive Trish would be in bed. If she was that passionate in conversation, it followed that she'd be a regular vixen in bed.

Too bad he would never find out.

Why not? his charged-up and thoroughly frustrated hormones screamed.

Because Trish was also about permanence and happily ever after. Any fool could see that. That made the two of them as incompatible as oil and water, fire and ice. He would just have to keep reminding himself of that before he started something they'd both regret, something that proved to her that he deserved his reputation as a low-down scoundrel.

Chapter Seven

"The space was absolutely perfect," Trish enthused as she and Kelly curled up at opposite ends of the sofa and sipped on cups of chamomile tea later that night. Despite the difference in their ages, Trish felt as comfortable with the older woman as she would have with one of her friends from home. She certainly felt more comfortable than she would have with her own mother.

"Then you think you might actually stay?" Kelly asked, her expression neutral, as if for once she didn't want to influence Trish's decision.

"I'm definitely considering it," Trish said. "I love the town. I think it would be a great place to raise Laura. I am a little worried about chasing Willetta off, but she swears she's ready for the move to Arizona."

"And Hardy? What did he have to say about this?"

Trish's exuberance faded. "He didn't say a whole lot, at least not about the store. I doubt we'll be seeing all that much of each other." She couldn't hide the note of regret that crept into her voice, but it perplexed her. How could she regret not seeing a man who embodied everything she despised? What sort of perversity had her wishing that things could have been different, that he could have been different?

"Why on earth not?" Kelly demanded. "You two didn't have a fight, did you?"

Trish shook her head. "Let's just say tonight was an eye-opening experience."

"In what way?"

"Well, I'd heard bits and pieces of the gossip, of course," she began.

Kelly cut her off. "You can't believe everything you hear. You ought to know that," she scolded.

"Oh, he all but admitted that he was a total scoundrel where women are concerned. And seeing him in action tonight—he even flirted with Willetta, for heaven's sakes—listening to him talk about how he feels about women and relationships, I realized he's just not for me, that's all," she declared defensively. "I've been there, done that."

"Oh, for heaven's sakes," Kelly said impatiently. "He's exactly like Jordan was, searching for something without even realizing it. It's because he's never met the right woman. The minute he does, he'll settle right down."

"What's the saying? You can't expect a leopard to change his spots? I think that applies," Trish said, ignoring the comparison Kelly was making to her own husband. "His attitude seems pretty entrenched to me. Besides, if I decide to open this store, I'll be too busy to even think about dating for a long, long time, much less about getting involved with anyone."

"But you do like him, don't you?" Kelly persisted. "The sparks were flying when he picked you up tonight."

"You can't trust chemistry," Trish said. "Sometimes it just blows up in a big puff of smoke and there's nothing left afterward."

"Don't you at least want to find out?" Kelly asked. "Do you want to spend the rest of your life wondering if you made a mistake, if you judged him too harshly?"

Trish regarded her curiously. "Why are you pushing this so hard?"

"No reason," Kelly said hurriedly. "I just like you. I like Hardy. I think you'd be good together. You already have an unbreakable bond."

"We're not back to the fact that he delivered Laura again, are we?"

"Well, you have to admit there's very little that's more intimate than that."

"It was an accident of fate, nothing more. I'm grateful. End of subject."

Kelly sighed. "If you say so."

"I do," Trish said very firmly. Her expression brightened. "Now let's talk about something I do want. Do you think it's too late to call your father-in-law and tell him I'm interested in the property?''

Kelly grinned. ''For news like this, it's never too late to call Harlan. He'll want to rush right over and get you to sign the papers.''

''Well, maybe that part can wait till morning, but let's at least tell him not to rent it out from under me.''

''Oh, believe me, I doubt there is any chance that would happen,'' Kelly said wryly. ''He has his heart set on having you stay right here.''

Trish hesitated, feeling that renewed sense of walking into a trap that she'd experienced earlier when she'd discovered that Harlan owned the property. ''Why would he feel so strongly about that? We've barely even met.''

''Oh, for a man known for his business acumen, Harlan makes totally impulsive decisions when it comes to people. He's taken an interest in you, and that's that.''

She handed Trish the portable phone and recited the number.

Harlan Adams answered with a booming greeting, despite the late hour.

''Sir, it's Trish Delacourt. I hope I'm not disturbing you.''

''No, indeed. I was hoping you'd call. What did you think of the store? Does it suit you?''

''It's wonderful. And the rent—''

''We can negotiate, if you think it's too high.''

Trish laughed. ''No, it's fine. If you'll have the

papers drawn up, I'll sign them in the morning. I'd like a year's lease, if that's okay.''

"Make it five," he countered. "We'll lock in the rent. Takes that long to see if a business will thrive. Can't be opening and closing after a few months, just when folks are discovering you're there."

A five-year commitment, Trish thought warily. Could she do that? Should she? An image of Hardy popped up. He was already invading her thoughts entirely too frequently, despite all those firm declarations she'd just made to Kelly. What if she couldn't keep him at bay? What if she let her hormones overrule her head and got another nasty taste of reality as she had with Jack? Would she want to stay in a town like Los Piños where she was bound to keep right on bumping into him?

"I'll give you a release clause," Harlan offered, as if sensing her uncertainty and very likely guessing the reason for it. "Something important comes up and you need to take off, you send me a letter and that will be that. Deal?"

She'd never get a better one, she realized. And a five-year lease at the terms he'd offered ensured that her overhead would remain stable until the store was on a sound financial footing.

"Deal," she agreed.

"Then you come on up to the house in the morning and we'll lock it in," he said. "Bring the baby, if you like. Nothing makes my day like cuddling a little one for a bit. Come for breakfast. Only way I get anything decent is if we're having company. Otherwise, my wife feeds me bran flakes and a banana every single day. You can help me sneak a cup of real coffee, too.''

Trish grinned at the thought of a powerful man like Harlan Adams having to sneak around behind his wife's back to get anything. She suspected he enjoyed the grumbling as much as he savored the occasional victory.

"I'll be there," she agreed.

"Eight o'clock too early?"

"Perfect."

"I'll see you then, young lady. I'll be looking forward to it."

Done, she thought with a little sigh of satisfaction as she hung up. By this time tomorrow she would be on her way to being back in business and settling in Los Piños for the foreseeable future. It seemed that fate had known what it was up to when she'd been stranded nearby.

"Daddy wants you to stop by the house this morning," Cody told Hardy when he found him in the bunkhouse dining room at seven-thirty, taking a break between chores.

"Why?" Hardy asked, genuinely perplexed. It wasn't as if he and Harlan Adams were buddies. And if it had something to do with ranch business, Cody would be passing along the orders.

"Far be it from me to question my father's motives," Cody said. "He works in mysterious ways, but he is still the boss around here. If he wants to see you, that's all that matters to me."

Hardy had a sinking sensation in the pit of his

stomach that the command performance had nothing to do with the ranch and everything to do with his personal life. He also knew there wasn't a snowball's chance in hell he could wriggle out of going.

"What time?" he asked with a resigned sigh.

"Eight," Cody said. "You might as well take off and head up to the main house now. The sooner you get it over with, the sooner you can get back to work."

"If you need me—"

Cody chuckled. "Oh, no. I'm not taking the blame for you not showing up. Obviously Daddy has some bee in his bonnet that concerns you."

Hardy heaved an even deeper sigh and headed for his pickup. When he reached the main house, Janet Adams answered his knock.

Harlan's wife was a handsome woman. With her high cheekbones and black hair streaked now with gray, there was no mistaking her Native American heritage. She carried herself as regally as a queen. One look at him, though, had her shaking her head, her expression amused. "I should have known," she murmured.

"Known what?" Hardy demanded, perplexed.

"You'll find out soon enough. He's expecting you. He's in the dining room having breakfast."

"I can wait till he's finished."

"Heavens, no. He wants you to come right on in and join the party, I'm sure," she said, that twinkle back in her dark brown eyes.

She led the way to the dining room, then gestured for him to go in. "If you need rescuing, give me a call," she said in an exaggerated whisper as she turned and walked away.

Only then did Hardy hear the voices, one deep and masculine, the other feminine and familiar. A baby's whimpers counterpointed the other two. So, he thought, that's what this was about. Harlan had set him up...again.

Before he could beat a hasty retreat, the sneaky old man caught sight of him.

"There you are," he boomed. "Come on in, son. Grab yourself some breakfast."

"I wouldn't want to intrude," Hardy said, his gaze locked on Trish and the baby even as he spoke to Harlan. Patches of color blossomed in her cheeks, proving that she, too, had been caught by surprise.

"I invited you, didn't I? Now get some food before it gets cold and have a seat. We have some planning to do."

"We do?" Hardy and Trish said in unison.

"Of course we do," the old man said, undaunted by their reaction. "If Trish here expects to get her store up and running soon, there's a lot of work to be done."

Trish's gaze shot from Hardy to Harlan Adams. "Sir, with all due respect, any work that's to be done is my responsibility."

"I'm the landlord," Harlan countered. "I can't have you moving in when the place is a mess, can I? Now I've been thinking. You'll want it painted, of course, maybe some bookshelves built in, a counter for your cash register. What else?"

Trish looked stunned. She also looked as if she

were about to blow a gasket. Apparently Harlan Adams was unaware that she'd left Houston because another domineering man—her father—had been intent on taking over her life and making all of her decisions for her.

"Mr. Adams," she began, her chin lifting defiantly.

"Harlan, young lady. I thought we'd settled that."

"Mr. Adams," she repeated just as firmly. "After Willetta moves out and I have a chance to go over the space more thoroughly, I will decide what needs to be done. Then I will make arrangements for the workmen. And I will pay for it."

Rather than being incensed by her declaration, Harlan let out a whoop of laughter. "Oh, you're a fiery one, aren't you? That's good." He went right on as if she hadn't just made her wishes perfectly clear. "Hardy, you're handy with a hammer and a saw, aren't you?"

"I suppose," he said, finally getting the full picture. "But I'm working for Cody with the cattle, sir. I can't just pick up and take off for however long it takes to get the store ready."

"You can if I say you can," Harlan Adams countered. "Old age still has some privileges around here." He frowned at Trish. "You got any objections to Hardy doing the work?"

Hardy could see her struggling with her reply. She was obviously torn between diplomacy and indignation, between practicality and a desire to keep Hardy at arm's length.

"None," she finally said with evident frustration.

"Good. That's settled then. Willetta will be out by the end of the week. I'll speak to Cody. You can start work down at the store on Monday, Hardy. Does that suit you, Trish?"

Looking as if she were surprised to be consulted, Trish responded tightly, "That will be fine."

"You just tell Hardy whatever you need, and he'll take care of it," Harlan said. "The bills will come to me."

"Absolutely not," Trish said forcefully. "These are my renovations."

"To my property," Harlan countered evenly.

Their gazes clashed, though Hardy was pretty sure he detected more humor than fire in the old man's. Hardy grinned at Trish.

"Give in gracefully," he advised. "You can't win."

"I most certainly can," she said, frowning at him. She turned back to Harlan. "If you insist on having your way on everything, I'm afraid this won't work out."

Harlan looked vaguely startled by the declaration, then held up the paper she'd just sighed. "We have a contract."

Her gaze met his evenly. "With an escape clause," she reminded him. "All it takes is a letter from me and the deal's off." She reached for pen and paper. "I can write it right now, if need be."

Harlan chuckled. "Okay, you can have it your way. You pay the bills."

Trish looked pleased with the victory, but Hardy

had the distinct impression Harlan would have the last laugh. He suspected the bills would come in, just as she'd asked, but that not a one of them would reflect the market value of the purchases. He could hardly wait to see the fireworks when Trish received the first one.

Harlan stood up, walked over to the sideboard and picked up the pot of coffee sitting there. He had barely poured himself a cup, when Janet walked into the room.

"I saw that," she said, sliding the cup out of his reach.

"Woman, don't you have someplace to be?"

"Not since you made me give up my law practice so we could share our golden years," she replied sweetly.

"What's golden about 'em when a man can't even get a decent cup of coffee?" he grumbled, but his gaze was warm as it rested on her face. Something in Hardy's chest tightened just watching the two of them.

"I'd best be on my way," Hardy said, suddenly needing to be out of the room and away from Trish, away from Laura and away from the kind of glowing, unconditional love he knew he'd never experience.

"Wait," Trish said, drawing his gaze. "I'll come with you, so we can make some arrangements for next week."

"Whatever."

As they left, Hardy thought he heard Janet ask, "Satisfied?"

Something told him she wasn't referring to breakfast. He suspected she wanted to know if her husband thought his scheming had paid off.

"I'd say it's looking promising," he told her, confirming Hardy's guess. "Now come on over here beside me and make me forget about that coffee you're denying me."

Hardy chuckled. He turned and caught Trish's grin. Obviously she had caught the exchange as well.

"He's something, isn't he?" she asked.

"He's a sneaky meddler," Hardy contradicted, but without any real rancor.

"That's certainly true enough. I'm sorry about you getting roped into this. If I could have thought of a way out, I would have. I'm sure there are plenty of contractors I could have hired to do whatever work is needed at the store."

Her eagerness to rid herself of his company annoyed him, especially under the guise of consideration for his feelings. "I'll survive. I imagine you will, too. In the end, you'll have your bookstore. Isn't that what matters?"

"I suppose." She peered at him intently. "Hardy, do you regret ever suggesting that I stay here? I know you said it impulsively and then I ran with the idea. I've always been like that. If something sounds right to me, I do it. I don't always stop to consider all the ramifications. Just look at how I ended up here in the first place."

He shrugged. "What I think doesn't matter now, does it? You're staying."

"But you'd rather I go," she persisted. "Why?"

He had thought that was obvious. "Because of what just happened, for one thing. Harlan's not the kind to let go once he's gotten an idea into his head. He's settled on getting us together, and he won't rest until he's accomplished that."

"We don't have to go along with it," she pointed out as if she genuinely believed it was a simple choice. "We're adults. We both know what we want and what we don't."

What Hardy wanted right this minute, more than anything, was to kiss the woman who was staring at him so earnestly, the woman who actually believed they were in control of their own destiny. He wanted to wipe that certainty off her face. He wanted her to tremble in his arms with sensations she couldn't simply wish away because they were inconvenient.

And because he usually took what he wanted, he stepped closer. Before she could begin to guess what he had on his mind, he dipped his head low and brushed his lips over hers. It wasn't enough, not nearly enough, he thought, startled by the depth of his sudden need for more. He cupped a hand behind her head and kissed her again, ignoring her startled gasp, savoring the fact that it enabled him to dip his tongue into the sweetness of her mouth.

With the baby clutched tightly in her arms and trapped awkwardly between them, she swayed toward him. Hardy was pretty sure the earth tilted on its axis, that heaven opened up and welcomed him, when he'd been counting on hell.

It was Laura's whimpers that finally cut through

the sensations rocketing through him. Clasping Trish's shoulders to keep her steady, he took a step back and fought for control. She stared up at him, her expression dazed and dreamy. Two red patches appeared in her cheeks.

Then, in the blink of an eye, fury replaced bemusement. "You have one heck of a nerve," she declared furiously. "Just because you're doing me a favor, don't start thinking—"

Hardy cut her off before she could travel too far down that particular path. "I am not doing you a favor," he reminded her. "I am doing a job that my boss has requested that I do. That's it."

"All the more reason not to take advantage of the situation," she countered. "This is a business relationship. It's not personal."

"You call it whatever you like," he taunted. "Personally, I'm beginning to think the benefits outweigh the salary."

"I am not part of the deal," she insisted. "If I have to, I will tell Harlan that it's not working out and that I don't want you anywhere near the store. Then he'll want to know what you did to offend me." She let the threat trail off.

"And you'll say I kissed you?" Hardy suggested. "Darlin', believe me, that will make his day."

As acceptance of the truth washed over her, she sighed heavily. "I suppose you're right."

"So do we try to make this work?"

"We don't seem to have any choice." She scowled at him. "No more kisses, though, and that's final."

Hardy kept his expression sober and nodded dutifully. "No more kisses," he echoed, then grinned, "unless you ask real nicely."

"I won't ask."

"We'll see."

There wasn't a woman on earth he couldn't make want him if he put his mind to it. A little charm, an innocent caress or two, a careless wink. He'd have her right where he wanted her in forty-eight hours. Maybe less.

Then what? he wondered as she went stalking off toward her car, her back ramrod straight, her shoulders squared with singed pride. Would a few more kisses satisfy him? Was that the goal? Or did he want her in his bed, just like all the others who'd come so easily? Thinking of Trish as nothing more than another notch on his bedpost turned his stomach sour. She didn't deserve that. Laura's mother deserved better.

There was just one trouble with that. He didn't have better to give.

Chapter Eight

Unable to control her exuberance, Trish twirled around in the middle of her new store, then clapped her hands in delight.

The property was hers as of this morning, and it was going to be fantastic. She could envision every bookcase, made of a warm wood that would give the room a cozy feel when the fireplace was lit. Two comfortable chairs for reading were arranged in front of it. The chairs would be covered in a bright chintz and deep enough to snuggle into. An antique table in the same wood as the shelves would sit between the chairs, with porcelain teacups and a silver teapot that was always filled. Maybe she'd even learn to bake scones. And there would be fresh flowers in a small crystal vase.

Of course, there would be books, jamming the shelves, invitingly displayed on more antique tables, stacked high near the cash register for impulse sales. And while the atmosphere would be deliberately old-fashioned, there would be a state-of-the-art computer for tracking everything, including all the special orders and catalogue and Internet sales she anticipated.

Right now, however, the space looked more like a nightmare than her dream store. Willetta apparently hadn't done a thorough cleaning since the fifties. Maybe longer. The last paint job had been haphazard at best, doing nothing to conceal patches or fine cracks in the plaster. The floors, which had been a lovely oak once, had been dulled to near-black by years of wax and dirt building up. It was even more decrepit than the building she'd rented in Houston, and that had been a dump.

If it hadn't been her nature to be optimistic, Trish might have been appalled by the work that faced her. Instead, she drew in a deep breath and headed to the store for cleaning supplies.

She had virtually the whole weekend ahead of her. Kelly was looking after Laura and had promised to do so again after church on Sunday. Trish planned to make a lot of progress over the weekend so that the real work could get under way the instant Hardy showed up on Monday. The sooner he was finished and out of her hair, the better. That kiss had told her quite clearly just how dangerous a mix it would be for the two of them to be in the same room for long.

Therefore it was with no particular pleasure that

she spotted Hardy leaning against the side of his pickup in front of her store as she returned from her shopping. Struggling with her bags, she frowned at him.

"What are you doing here?"

"I came to help."

"You're not scheduled to start work until Monday."

"You're here, aren't you? There's work to be done, right?" he said, taking the bags from her before she could utter a protest.

"But—"

He sighed and faced her. "Trish, I am not going to throw you down on the floor and ravish you. Get that picture right out of your head."

Of course, as soon as he said it, that was all she could see. Heat stirred low in her belly as she imagined herself flat on the floor with Hardy's body on top of hers, with him buried inside her. Obviously her hormones didn't have the sense of a gnat.

"I was not worried about that," she insisted, unlocking the door and preceding him inside.

He surveyed her with a skeptical expression. "If you say so. Now what do you want done first?"

She wanted him to go.

But not nearly as much as she wanted him to stay, she concluded with regret. They could do the work together in half the time that it would take her alone. And having company always made work seem easier. It was just that his company promised to leave her feeling every bit as rattled and unsettled as that kiss they'd shared.

Just as she accepted that, she saw him heading for the door. ''You're leaving?'' she asked, fearing that her lack of a warm reception had finally daunted him.

He grinned. ''No, darlin', Don't go getting your hopes up. I don't scare off that easily. I'm going to get my radio out of the truck. We can't work without music.''

She stared at him. ''We can't?''

''Well, I suppose we could, but this will be better. There's a six-pack of beer in there for me and some sodas for you. And a bag of chips, a couple of sandwiches, apples, brownies. I'm not entirely certain, but there may be a pig in there ready to go on the barbeque.''

She was stunned. ''Hardy, we're not having a party.''

''Tell that to Kelly. She packed it all.''

She stared at him blankly. ''Kelly? When?''

''When I stopped by the house to see what you were up to. She told me you'd come into town. She sounded as if you'd gone off to work in a coal mine in some godforsaken land where no human had ever gone before. Before I knew it, I was carting bags of provisions out to the truck. She seemed to think we'll perish from hunger.''

Trish stared as he carted in a card table, two folding chairs and grocery bags every bit as bulging as he'd described.

''Maybe she was anticipating a blizzard,'' she joked weakly.

Or maybe she'd merely been hoping for one, a

doozy of a storm that would leave Trish trapped here with Hardy for a day or two. She peered into the bags and caught a whiff of the just-baked brownies, clearly still warm from the oven. Unable to resist, she snatched one from the package, then offered them to Hardy.

"Not just yet," he said. "Why don't you have a seat, enjoy your brownie and start bossing me around?"

With regret, she put her brownie aside and wiped her fingers on a napkin. "No, no, I'll get started, too."

He clasped her shoulders, nudged her toward a chair, then handed the chocolate square back to her. "Come on, boss lady, bark out some orders. You know you want to. There's not a woman alive who doesn't get a thrill from having a man at her beck and call."

"You'll do anything I want you to?" she asked speculatively.

His eyes widened. "Now that certainly sounds promising. What did you have in mind?"

"Nothing like that," she protested, guessing the wicked direction his thoughts had taken.

"Too bad. For a minute there, my heart almost stopped."

She regarded him with resignation. "You can't really help it, can you?"

"What?"

"Flirting."

"Why would I want to stop?" he asked. "It keeps things interesting."

"But it's all a game to you. Are you ever serious about anything?"

"Not if I can help it. We only get one shot at living. I figure it ought to be fun." He regarded her curiously. "What about you?"

She tried to think back to the last time she'd had fun without giving a thought to the consequences. "Fun has its place, I suppose."

He studied her thoughtfully. "How many times have you laughed today?"

The question threw her. "I have no idea. Why?"

"Because sharing laughter is almost as good as sex." He moved closer and touched a finger to the corner of her eyes. "When you laugh, when your eyes light up, I think I can see into your soul."

She shuddered as if his touch had been far more intimate. But it was his words, his unexpectedly poetic turn of phrase, not his touch, that stirred her deep inside where she'd vowed never again to let any man reach, especially not a glib charmer like Hardy.

A smile tugged at his lips. "I surprised you, didn't I? You figured me for a rough-and-tumble cowboy with nothing on his mind besides a quick roll in the hay."

"Of course not," she denied heatedly, because he was too close to the truth.

"Liar."

She didn't even try to defend herself. She just picked up a broom and turned away. She felt his hands on her shoulders, felt herself being turned until she faced him. His gaze settled on her gently, seriously.

"Trish, I'm going to warn you one time and one time only, don't underestimate me. I flirt because I enjoy it. I laugh because it's better than the alternative. But just when you think you know me, I guarantee, I'll surprise you."

She met his gaze evenly, felt another stirring of the heat that scared her and said quietly, "You already have."

He gave a little nod of satisfaction, then reached for the broom she held. "Then I suppose that's enough surprises for one morning." He winked at her. "I have to parcel them out or you'll start taking them for granted."

No, Trish thought, as he went to work. She had a feeling that after today she would never take anything about Hardy Jones for granted ever again.

Hardy had done his share of odd jobs over the years. He'd worked for a wide variety of bosses, some downright mean, some kind and patient, some demanding. But he'd never before worked for one who smelled of exotic spices and worked alongside him with nonstop chatter.

It seemed Trish was finally accepting his presence. Her nervous conversation, which didn't seem to require any response from him, suggested she might not be entirely comfortable with him yet, but she was clearly determined to make the best of it. He kept trying to get her to take it easy, reminding her that she'd just had a baby, that she needed to

rest, to eat a decent lunch. She sat only when he sat,
ate only when he ate.

Which meant that not very much got done. Hardy
took more breaks than the best union contract in the
country called for. He skipped the beer and drank
milk, just to set a good example. He snacked on
apples when he wanted chips. He claimed exhaustion and sat, when every fiber of his being cried out
to get the job done.

"What made you decide you wanted to run a
bookstore?" he asked as they sat side by side on the
floor, sipping milk and eating the last of the brownies, their backs pressed against the wall.

"I always loved to read," she said. "I could lose
myself in a book, go anywhere I wanted to go, be
somebody daring and adventurous."

He thought of her taking off and heading far from
home when she was about to have a baby. That
seemed pretty daring and adventurous to him. "You
didn't think of yourself as adventurous?"

She laughed. "Hardly. My father and my brothers
got to have all the adventures. From the moment I
was born, as the youngest child, the only girl, I was
put on a pedestal and pampered. I hated it. I wanted
to do what my brothers did. No, not exactly what
they did," she corrected. "I didn't especially want
to play football or get my nose broken in a fistfight,
but I wanted the freedom they had. Do you know
that I never came home from a date *not* to find my
father sitting up waiting for me when I came in?"

"A lot of fathers wait up for their daughters,"
Hardy said, not understanding the problem. He'd

been caught in a compromising kiss more times than he cared to recall, but it hadn't been the humiliating end of the world she was making it out to be. "Isn't it some sort of tradition?"

"But I was in my twenties," she said ruefully. "It was embarrassing. I tried to move out and get my own place, but he and my mother were so horrified I finally caved in and stayed home."

"How on earth did you ever manage to get—" He cut himself off before he could say it.

Trish slid a glance his way. "How did I get pregnant?"

He nodded.

"With Jack it was different, because he was the man my father had chosen for me. The apron strings were loosened. Everybody assumed that no harm could possibly come to me when I was with Jack. I'm sure they were stunned when they realized just how wrong they were. Then again, the thinking went, what did it matter? After all, we were going to be married, weren't we? When I put an end to that fantasy, that's when the trouble started."

"Surely by now you've made your point," he suggested.

"I doubt it. The Delacourts are stubborn to a fault. My father more so than any of us. Even if I'm gone for years, he'll probably keep Jack dangling on a string just in case I change my mind."

Hardy studied her expression. She was serious. "What does that say about him?"

"That he's a weak man," she said readily. "That

he wants what my father's holding just out of reach more than he cares about his self-respect.''

"The man's a fool.''

"Which one?''

"Both, now that you mention it. Your father for not trusting your instincts and Jack for not having any gumption. I'd have told your father what he could do a long time ago,'' he declared, then captured her gaze. "And I would never have let you get away.''

He realized even as he said the words that a part of him didn't want to let her go even after knowing her so briefly, even without sleeping with her. At the same time he also knew that he would eventually let her go—would send her away, in fact—because that was what he did. He was every bit as much a fool as Jack Grainger.

Because he didn't like the direction his thoughts had taken, he stood up and grabbed sandpaper and spackle and went to work on smoothing and patching the walls. The country music station played songs that echoed his mood, love-gone-wrong tunes that seemed to mirror the way his future was laid out.

In the past he'd heard the sad words, sung along with them, in fact, but he hadn't related to them because he'd never lost a woman he loved. Now he was faced with the prospect of losing a woman he'd never even given himself a chance to love. Regrets, something he rarely indulged in, taunted him.

He glanced over and caught Trish trying to mimic his actions. She had climbed onto one of the folding chairs and was reaching high to sand a sloppy patch job. The movement lifted her breasts and pulled her sweater loose from her jeans, displaying a sliver of bare skin. His mouth went dry at the sight.

Then she rose on tiptoe, and the unstable chair wobbled beneath her, throwing her off balance. Barely in the nick of time he realized that she was about to topple off. Thankful for his lightning-quick reflexes, he caught her in midair and pulled her tight against his chest.

"Oh, dear," she murmured, as her gaze clashed with his.

He saw the precise second when fright gave way to an awareness that their bodies were pressed intimately together. He felt her skin heat, felt his own temperature soar. He could feel her breasts heaving with each startled gasp of breath she took.

Bad idea, he told himself firmly, but he couldn't seem to make himself release her. She felt too good, fit too perfectly against him. And he couldn't resist holding her just a little longer to see precisely what she would do after the initial shock of her near fall wore off.

He saw the muscle work in her throat, felt her pulse fluttering wildly beneath his touch, but she didn't jerk away, didn't struggle to get out of the compromising position. In fact, she was so still, her gaze so watchful, he gathered that she intended to leave the next move up to him. Anticipation simmered between them.

It would have been so easy, so natural to kiss the parted lips just inches from his own. For an instant he actually considered it, even ran his tongue over his own lips in readiness.

But then he saw the predictability of it, knew that that was precisely what she was expecting. Better, he concluded, to be disappointed himself at one missed opportunity and surprise her with his restraint.

Because he wasn't a saint, he allowed her body to slide slowly along his until her feet touched the floor. Every inch of him was aware of the contact, ached with it. Still, once he was assured she was steady enough, he released her and deliberately backed away.

"Are you okay?" he asked, jamming his hands in his pockets to keep from reaching for her again.

"Fine," she said unsteadily, her eyes filled with confusion, and maybe just a hint of relief.

It was the latter that reassured him he'd made the right choice. He knew he could get to her with a kiss, knew that the chemistry was explosive enough to lead to seduction when the time was right. But not yet, not when it would only prove every single rotten opinion she already held about him. Having the reputation of a womanizer had never especially bothered him before, because his conscience was clear when it came to each of the women he'd dated. Having Trish think the worst bothered him for reasons he wasn't sure he really wanted to explore.

Slowly, and again with careful deliberation, he turned his back on her and retrieved his sandpaper and spackle. He went back to work as if the incident had never taken place, as if his nerves weren't jumbled and his pulse weren't racing.

"Hardy?"

"Hmm?"

"What just happened here?"

He bit back a grin at the irritation in her voice. "Nothing, why?"

"It didn't feel like nothing."

He glanced over his shoulder to see that she was sitting on the chair now, regarding him with a perplexed expression.

"Oh?" he said innocently. "What did it feel like?"

She peered at him intently. "You honestly didn't notice anything?"

"Darlin', you're going to have to be more precise than that. Notice what?"

She held up her hands in a vulnerable, helpless gesture that would have drawn another smile, if he hadn't figured that was a sure way to get clobbered by a hammer.

"Never mind."

He shrugged. "Whatever." He forced his attention back to the job.

"Hardy?"

"Yes."

"Why didn't you kiss me just now?"

He swallowed a laugh at the plaintive note in her voice. Keeping his expression perfectly serious, he met her gaze. "You told me no more kisses. That was the deal, wasn't it? I never go back on my word.

Haven't I told you that?'' He studied her an instant. ''What about you? Have you changed your mind?''

''No, of course not,'' she said impatiently, then sighed. ''I suppose you think I'm totally perverse.''

He grinned. ''No, what I think is that you don't know your own mind. Let's face it, you've had a bad experience with a jerk. You don't trust your own judgment. I can wait.''

She eyed him warily. ''Wait? For what?''

''For you to admit you want me.''

Her expression froze. ''Want you?'' she echoed as his very explicit response sank in. ''Oh, no, you are definitely wrong about that. I absolutely, positively do not want you. No way. You can just get that idea right out of your head.''

He shrugged as if it made no difference to him one way or the other. ''Oh well, maybe I was wrong.''

''You were. Absolutely.''

''Whatever you say.''

''Hardy, I am serious. Don't go getting any ideas. I don't do flings.''

''Of course not. No ideas,'' he echoed. ''I'm taking you at your word.''

Her gaze narrowed as if she sensed a trick, but she finally gave a little nod of satisfaction. ''Good.''

''Besides, you're a blunt, straightforward woman. I'm sure you'll let me know if you change your mind,'' he suggested.

''I won't change my mind.''

''Okay, then. It's settled. Can I get back to work now?''

"Of course." She reached for the bag of chips and began munching them as if she hadn't eaten for a month. After a couple of minutes she stared at them as if she had no idea how they'd gotten into her hand. Scowling, she dropped the bag as though she'd just discovered it was filled with worms.

"Anything wrong?" he asked.

"Not a thing," she said firmly. "I think I'll go sweep out the storeroom."

He grinned as she backed out of the room, carrying the broom in front of her as if it was meant to ward off any unwanted advances.

Oh, she wanted him, all right. Hardy recognized the signs. Unfortunately he had no idea what he should—or dared—to do about it. He had a feeling that the longer he went on playing with fire, the greater the odds were that someone was going to get burned. He had an even stronger, even more troubling feeling that this time—for the first time in the history of his social life—it could be him.

Chapter Nine

Hardy headed straight for Garden City the minute he and Trish wrapped up work on Saturday. He needed a drink. He needed a heavy dose of uncomplicated flirting. He needed to go home with a woman who wouldn't wake up in the morning with expectations.

Of course, as usual lately, what he needed and what he got were two different things.

Harlan Patrick was seated at the bar, listening raptly as his wife performed her latest song in a test run before a very friendly audience. In this one, the romance had a happy ending and the tune was upbeat, reflecting the state of their marriage. Hardy was a whole lot more comfortable hearing about broken hearts. Those songs reaffirmed his cynical conviction that real love didn't exist.

Harlan Patrick gestured toward the vacant bar stool next to him. "Join me. I'll buy you a beer."

Hardy figured the beer would come with strings attached. Harlan Patrick would probably waste no time pumping him for information about Trish and the state of the romance everyone in the Adams clan was hoping for.

"Sure, why not?" he agreed, hiding his reluctance. Hoping for at least a temporary distraction, he added, "Laurie sounds good."

Harlan Patrick's expression brightened. "She always does."

"The song's a little different from her usual."

"Yeah. She's worried about it, too," he admitted. "She thinks happiness is boring and that she's losing her edge. I keep telling her she could sing the phone book and her fans would be ecstatic."

"I'm sure she finds that reassuring," Hardy commented.

"No, as a matter of fact, she gives me the same 'oh sure' look you're giving me."

"Does she have another concert tour coming up?"

As Hardy expected, Harlan Patrick's expression soured.

"Not for a few more months, but that's too soon for me. I'm hoping there's enough time for me to persuade her to do a television special instead."

"You really hate it when she's on the road, don't you?"

Harlan Patrick nodded. "And now with two kids, there's even more reason for her to stay put, but I learned my lesson a few years back. If touring makes her happy, I'll figure out a way to live with it."

Laurie wrapped up her set, strolled over and put her arms around Harlan Patrick's neck. "Hey, cowboy, buy a girl a drink?"

"You've got it," he said, brightening at once.

Laurie grinned at Hardy. "So how much work did you and Trish actually get done today?"

"I see the White Pines grapevine is alive and well," Hardy noted, ignoring the question.

"Indeed. Between Kelly, who packed the lunch, and Sharon Lynn, who crept next door to peek in the windows, we pretty much know everything," Laurie said with unrepentant glee.

"Then why ask me?"

"Confirmation, of course. Plus spin. These secondhand reports lack all the juicy details."

"Too bad," Hardy grumbled. "Because I'm not talking."

Harlan Patrick regarded him speculatively. "Is that so? I wonder why?"

"I never kiss and tell," Hardy said.

"Of course you do," his friend contradicted. "Why do you think the guys in the bunkhouse wait up for you? They're living vicariously through you."

"So, spill it," Laurie said. "Do you like her?"

Now there was a dangerous question. Hardy considered his response carefully. "Of course I like her. She's a very nice woman."

"Nice?" Laurie made a face. "What a disgustingly lukewarm description. She's beautiful."

"You'll get no argument from me about that."

"Then you are attracted to her?" she gloated, putting her own spin on things.

"I never said—"

"Give it up," Harlan Patrick advised. "Once these women get an idea into their heads, you'll only make yourself crazy trying to convince them otherwise."

"I thought your grandfather was the one I needed to watch out for," Hardy said, unable to keep a plaintive note out of his voice. At the rate the number of matchmakers was multiplying, he might as well go out and buy the blasted engagement ring.

"Where do you think they get their inspiration?" Harlan Patrick retorted. "He won't live forever and he's making darn sure that others share his skill."

Hardy noticed the amorous Rita watching him from across the room, her expression hopeful. He knew that a simple nod of his head would bring her over, knew precisely where it would lead. That was what he had wanted when he'd walked through the door, simple, uncomplicated sex.

Unfortunately all this talk about Trish had cooled his desire. He knew he'd never get her image out of his head, no matter how wickedly clever some other woman might be. He sighed with regret and forced his gaze back to Laurie and Harlan Patrick. He noted that the man was regarding him with undisguised sympathy.

"You going back into town to help her tomorrow?" Harlan Patrick asked.

"I imagine," Hardy said reluctantly.

"Maybe we should go, too," Laurie suggested. "We can make a party of it. I'll call Val and the others first thing in the morning."

Terrific, Hardy thought. Not only would he have to contend with the frustration of being around Trish without doing anything about the attraction that was building between them, but he'd have avid witnesses to his resulting discomfort.

Maybe he just wouldn't go. After all, if she had all that willing help, why did she need him? He wasn't on her payroll until Monday. He could stay at the ranch and do something physical, something that would wear him out, something that would drive any and all thoughts of Trish Delacourt and her sexy little body and vulnerable eyes out of his head. Then he could take an icy shower for good measure. Maybe if he tamed every last trace of lust, he could get through the next week without losing his mind.

The store was crawling with people, so many that they were getting in each other's way, then laughing good-naturedly about the ensuing chaos. Trish stood back and watched the various members of the Adams clan scrubbing floors, washing down walls, patching plaster and teasing each other with an affection she envied. Only Kelly was missing. She'd stayed home with Laura once again.

And Hardy, of course. Trish's gaze shot to the

door each time it swung open, but he hadn't shown up. She kept telling herself it didn't matter, that he wasn't obligated to be here today, but she missed him more than she wanted to admit.

"Looking for anyone in particular?" Laurie asked, sneaking up beside her.

"Of course not," Trish denied, fully aware of the heat that scalded her cheeks.

"Well, if you are looking for Hardy, I think I'm responsible for him not being here."

"Why on earth would you think that?"

"To tell you the truth, I might have scared him off," Laurie admitted. "He was in Garden City last night."

"Oh, really?" Trish said. "With a woman?"

The telling question popped out before she could stop herself.

Laurie grinned. "No, alone. Anyway, we got to talking after one of my sets. I suppose I was prying a little too much. It might have made him skittish."

"Prying? About what?"

"The two of you."

"There is no two of us," she said vehemently.

Laurie chuckled. "Funny. He denied it, too. Almost as emphatically as you just did. Makes me wonder, especially since you seem to be so fascinated by whether or not he was by himself."

"What exactly are you wondering about?" Trish asked warily.

"Why you're both protesting so hard. What would be wrong with the two of you getting together?"

"Hardy is not interested in a serious relationship," Trish said. "He likes chasing women, plural. I've just gotten out of one relationship with a man of similar inclinations. I don't intend to jump back into that particular frying pan."

Laurie nodded, her expression thoughtful. "Yes, I can see how that could be a problem. Then just be friends. Nothing wrong with that, is there?"

"I don't think a man like Hardy is capable of being just friends with a woman."

"Try it. He might surprise you."

Trish recalled that he had said much the same thing. "I'm at the point in my life where the fewer surprises I have, the better."

Laurie looked horrified. "Oh, don't say that. If there are no surprises, you're settling. You're not living. Trust me, you'll be bored to tears in no time."

"After the past few months, boredom sounds downright refreshing," Trish countered. She chuckled at Laurie's downcast expression. "Don't look so glum. My life is exactly the way I want it to be right now. I have a beautiful baby girl. I'm about to open a new business. What more could I possibly want?"

"Someone to share it all with," Laurie suggested, clearly undaunted.

"I have all of you," Trish said. "I feel as if I've found a whole slew of new friends."

"Well, of course, you have, but—"

"No buts," Trish insisted. "This is for the best."

The door opened, and her gaze swung toward it.

Laurie chuckled at her obvious disappointment when it turned out to be Val and Slade.

"You're deluding yourself," Laurie told her with undisguised amusement. "But far be it from me to destroy the illusion. If you don't mind, though, I think I'll just sit back and see what develops. My money's on love."

Between the conversation with Laurie and a flurry of innuendoes from every other person who dropped by, Trish was downright cranky by the time she got back to Jordan and Kelly's. She was also convinced that she needed to put some distance between herself and the meddling Adamses.

She headed straight for the portable bassinet Kelly had set up in the living room and picked up her daughter. Thankfully there was at least one person she could count on who wouldn't be badgering her with questions about Hardy.

"How's mama's darling girl?" she asked the sleepy baby.

"She's been a little angel," Kelly assured her. "No fussing. Drank every last drop of her bottle and went right back to sleep. I kept hoping she'd wake up so I could play with her, but no such luck."

"Thanks for taking care of her."

"It was my pleasure. Besides, I had some help."

"Oh?"

"Hardy dropped by."

Trish stared. "He did?"

"Never really said what he wanted, but I assumed it was to see your precious little one. He fed her and rocked her as if he'd been doing it all his life. They had quite a chat. I tried eavesdropping, but he kept his voice too low for me to hear,'' she said, obviously disgruntled.

"Are you sure he didn't come by to see Jordan or something?'' Trish asked.

"Nope. He seemed to know that Jordan was out of town and that you were at the store.'' She grinned. "I'll admit, Laura was wailing and I sort of shoved her into his arms while I fixed her bottle, but when I came back into the room, he was cooing at her like a proud papa. He settled her right down. You should have seen him with her. It would have melted your heart.''

Trish didn't doubt it. She sank into a chair. What on earth had possessed him to drop by? she wondered. Apparently the fact that he'd delivered Laura had created a more powerful bond than she'd realized, not just with her, but with her daughter. Just as obvious was the fact that he didn't want her to know about it. He'd deliberately chosen to come by when he'd known she wouldn't be there, as if he feared her making too much out of whatever attention he paid to the baby.

She glanced away from the baby's face and realized Kelly was staring at her with a puzzled expression.

"You're not upset because he spent time with Laura, are you?''

"No, of course not. I'm just surprised.''

"How did things go at the store? Did you get a lot of work done?''

"Yes.'' When everyone hadn't been busy prying

into her love life, she thought wryly. "Everyone was wonderful. But I can't go on depending on all of you for everything. I need to start making my own plans for living arrangements."

"Absolutely not," Kelly said. "There's plenty of room here, and we love having you. Once you get the store up and running, if you want to find your own place we'll help you. In the meantime, I'm right here to look after Laura while you work. It's winter, so there's less for me to do on the ranch. I always get a little antsy this time of year. I'm glad of the distraction. Besides, if you moved now, you'd have to find a sitter. You can't take Laura with you. She has no business being there while you're painting."

"I suppose you're right," Trish admitted. "Staying here for the time being does make sense."

"Of course it does. So, that's the end of that." Kelly peered at her. "What brought that up out of the blue, anyway? Too many nosy people trying to run your life today?"

Trish grinned at the assessment. "Something like that."

"Ignore us. No one means any harm. We just can't help ourselves."

"One person I could ignore. Maybe even two," Trish argued. "But there are so many of you."

"And we're all right," Kelly teased. "Still doesn't mean you have to listen to us. Tune us out. Make your own decisions. Tell us to take a flying leap, if it suits you. We won't be insulted. In fact, we're used to it."

"Yes, I imagine you are," Trish said, thinking

that however many insults had been hurled at them over the years, they remained steadfastly undaunted when it came to meddling.

"Can I ask one last nosy question before I quit for the night?"

Trish regarded her with amusement. "Could I stop you?"

"Probably not."

"Then go for it."

"Are you even the teeniest bit tempted by Hardy? I mean the man is seriously gorgeous. Even I'm not too old to recognize that."

Trish sighed heavily and admitted, "I'd have to be dead not to be."

Kelly grinned. "Then we're not wasting our time. Good."

Too late, Trish realized that she'd just offered encouragement to an entire clan of matchmakers. Now they'd never in a million years believe that their cause was hopeless.

Hardy finally discovered a serious flaw in Trish. When it came to choosing the wood for her bookshelves, she couldn't make a decision to save her soul. Unfortunately he found her indecision more amusing than annoying.

She hadn't been satisfied with the selection at a local lumber company, so he'd suggested a trip to Garden City. Now they were surrounded by samples of maple, pine, oak, cherry and mahogany. She rubbed her fingers over the grain. She sniffed deeply, as if she might be swayed by the fragrance alone. She studied the prices, punched numbers into her little pocket calculator and noted them on the paper they'd brought with measurements. Then she sighed and went through the same routine all over again.

Hardy lounged against a pile of two-by-fours and watched her. When he could stand it no longer, he asked, "Mind if I make a suggestion?"

She blinked and stared at him as if she'd just realized he was along. "Sure."

"Buy the less expensive wood and stain it to get the effect you want. I'm assuming what you're going for is something warm. You keep gravitating toward the cherry. A few cans of stain and a little work and you'll have the next best thing."

Her expression brightened. Before he realized her intention, she threw her arms around him and gave him a smacking kiss on the cheek. "You're a genius! I want the cherry so badly I can taste it, but the cost would really eat into my budget. Do you really think the stain won't look cheap?"

Hardy couldn't think at all. That little kiss-and-run gesture of hers had left him reeling. All the hard work he'd done over the weekend to make himself believe that what he felt was nothing more than infatuation was wasted.

"Hardy?"

He swallowed hard. "It'll look fine," he assured her. "I'm sure there are samples over there with the stains, so you can get an idea of how it would look."

"Of course," she said, and darted off.

He drew in a deep breath and tried to reclaim his

composure before he followed her to the next aisle. She was already holding up little blocks of wood and examining them this way and that. When she caught sight of him, she beamed, and his heart did another of those annoying little flips.

"Look," she enthused. "It will work, don't you think? You can't tell this isn't really cherry."

"That's the idea," he pointed out. "If it didn't work, no one would do it."

She frowned at him. "Okay, smarty. Just order the stain and the wood," she said, handing him the sheet with their measurements before bounding off.

"Where are you going?"

"To see about renting a sander and polisher to refinish those floors. They're going to gleam by the time we're done."

Hardy seriously doubted that anything short of sandblasting would clean the grime off those floors, but he shrugged and went to order the lumber. By the time he'd finished, Trish was at the checkout counter with her own purchases, which included two huge concrete flower planters.

"What are those for?" he asked.

"On either side of the front door. I'll fill them with different flowers, depending on the season. They're going to deliver the potting soil with the lumber."

Hardy had never been able to see the sense in planting and tending flowers that served no useful purpose. A garden was meant to be productive. All that work ought to result in tomatoes, peppers, corn and beans, at the very least. It was just one more difference between them. Practicality versus day-dreams.

"Do you have a problem with flowers?" she asked, regarding him with amusement.

"Not on principle," he said. "Besides, you're the one who's going to have to take care of them."

"Exactly," she said, then wrote a check for the staggering total without even batting an eye.

Even after they were in his truck, Hardy couldn't shake his unease about the amount of money she was throwing around. "Don't think I haven't noticed that you're paying as you go, just so Harlan can't get at the bills. Are you sure you're not spending too much on fixing the place up?"

"Absolutely not. It has to have the right atmosphere from the very beginning. You can't make up for a poor first impression."

Hardy wondered about that. He and Trish hadn't exactly gotten off on the right foot, but he'd pretty much forgotten her snippy attitude, attributing it to temporary stress. Now he couldn't seem to shake the effect of all her good points.

Of course, the same couldn't be said for her. She'd been holding tight to her first impression of him, probably because it was getting reinforced at every turn.

"Obviously you know what you're doing," he said eventually. "What's next?"

"Are there any antique shops nearby?"

"Probably downtown. That's the historic district. I seem to recall passing a few in that area."

"Show me," she commanded as if he were a tour guide she'd hired for the day.

He scowled at her. "You know, darlin', you might not have liked being the pampered baby in the family, but you seem to have developed a real fondness for behaving like a princess."

She stopped dead in her tracks. "Excuse me?"

"The high-and-mighty tone," he explained.

"You're the one who asked what I wanted to do next."

"So I did. Forget it."

"No. I think we should talk about this. Aren't you the one who insisted that this whole project was strictly business, that you were doing a job, not a favor?"

He didn't like where she was heading with this one little bit. "Yes. So?"

"So that makes you my employee for all intents and purposes."

"And you think that means you get to order me around like some loyal subject?" he demanded, ignoring the fact that he'd told her to do that very thing on Saturday.

"Of course not," she said, her complexion flushed. She heaved a sigh. "Hardy, sometimes I don't know what to make of you. I have no idea what you really want."

Hearing her confusion, it was his turn to sigh. "Sometimes I'm not sure myself."

He gazed into eyes the same shade of blue as the brilliant winter sky. "Except for this," he murmured, bending his head to capture her lips beneath his.

Oblivious to their surroundings, oblivious to everything except the feel of satin under his mouth, he threw himself into the kiss.

He didn't touch her, didn't put a hand on her, but the swirl of heat from the kiss alone was enough to melt steel. His blood roared through his veins. His heart pounded. The mysterious, exotic scent of her teased his senses. He sank into the kiss, dragging her with him until they were both unsteady, both all but gasping for breath.

Her eyes were wide with shock when he finally pulled back. Her lips were swollen with the look of a mouth that had just been thoroughly, devastatingly devoured.

"Oh, sweet heaven," she whispered, touching her trembling fingers to her lips as if she couldn't quite believe how they had betrayed her.

"This isn't supposed to...it can't be..."

Hardy grinned at her incoherence. "Darlin', I know you're quite a talker, but I don't think you can talk this away. Words aren't going to change anything. And I don't think *supposed to* has anything to do with it."

Her gaze narrowed. He caught the quick rise of temper.

"Are you pleased with yourself because you managed to get a physical reaction out of me?" she demanded.

That was one way of putting how he felt, Hardy supposed, but he sensed that he'd be smarter to deny it. "I enjoyed kissing you, there's no question about that," he said carefully. "You going to deny you enjoyed it?"

She looked as if she wanted to, looked as if the denial were on the tip of her tongue, but she was too innately honest to pull off the lie.

"Okay, it was a great kiss."

"Just like the last one," he suggested.

She scowled. "Don't push it. The point is, a kiss is just a momentary phenomenon. In our case it also represents a lapse in judgment."

Hardy couldn't help it. He chuckled. "You are so cute when you get all prim and earnest."

Practically trembling with rage, she stared at him. "This is not a game, Hardy Jones. I will not be another notch on your bedpost. If that's what you've got in mind, you can take your little innuendoes and your flirting and your help and go straight to hell."

She flounced off before he could snap his mouth closed. She was two blocks away before he caught up with her. He'd figured it would take at least that long for her to cool down and listen to reason.

When he fell into step beside her, he noted that her color was still high, her mood still precarious. He opted for silence. Maybe after another block or two, he'd think of something to say to soothe her ruffled feathers.

"That's not what this is about," he finally said quietly.

She kept her gaze straight ahead and remained stoically silent.

"To tell you the honest truth, I'm not sure what

it's about," he admitted. "I've broken every single one of my rules where you're concerned."

She finally stole a glance at him. "Oh?"

"You're vulnerable and innocent," he began.

"I'm an unwed mother," she pointed out. "Hardly innocent."

"A technicality," he insisted. "In my book you're innocent. And you have a daughter, who could be hurt if we don't play by the rules."

She regarded him with confusion. "Whose rules are we talking about now? Yours?"

"No, society's."

"I had no idea you even knew what those were."

"Oh, I know. I just prefer to ignore most of them." He met her gaze. "I can't with you. You come from a good family. You have permanence and happily ever after written all over you. I'm a ranch hand who doesn't think much farther ahead than tomorrow. I'm all about living in the moment. We're not suited."

To his chagrin, she nodded. "I agree."

"Then why can't I keep my hands off you?" he asked, genuinely perplexed. "Why can't I get you out of my head? Usually I steer so far away from women like you, we're practically not even in the same state."

"Probably because you know we'd be a disaster, which makes me forbidden. People always want what they can't have, what's bad for them. It's just a totally irrational fascination, one we just have to try harder to nip in the bud."

"You think so?"

"I know so," she said with confidence. "So now that that's clear, we can just settle down and be friends. Deal?"

"Friends," Hardy echoed dutifully. He didn't even need the impact of that last kiss to tell him that they had a snowball's chance in hell of pulling that off.

Chapter Ten

Friendship should have suited Trish just fine. It was what she had asked for, wasn't it? And Hardy was throwing himself into the role with total dedication. He hadn't so much as glanced straight into her eyes, much less uttered a teasing remark to her for the past two weeks.

He also went to great lengths to avoid touching her. If he handed her something, he released it practically before she could get a grip on it, just to ensure that their fingers didn't brush. He was prompt, cheerful and helpful. She couldn't fault him for that. The store was taking shape a whole lot faster than she'd anticipated. In fact, she suspected he couldn't finish the job fast enough.

So why was she so disgruntled at the end of every

day? Why did she feel as if she'd lost something precious?

Because she was a ninny, that's why. Friendship was what she'd asked for. Friendship was what she'd gotten. If she wasn't satisfied, then it was her own fault.

She glanced over at Hardy who'd stripped off his shirt to display a devastatingly muscular back and shoulders that a body builder would have envied. He was bent over a sawhorse, cutting through a piece of lumber for the last set of shelves. Staring at his gleaming flesh, at the bunching of his muscles, her mouth went dry. His tush wasn't bad, either, she concluded when she shifted her gaze in that direction.

Sweet heaven, what was happening to her? She was turning into some sort of sex-crazed female. Maybe it was all the hormonal ups and downs her body had been through lately. She seized on that explanation like a lifeline. That had to be it. It couldn't possibly be personal when they had decided, very clearly, very plainly, that friendship was all that was in the cards for the two of them.

"Trish?"

She snapped back to reality and met his gaze. Was she mistaken or was there a wicked, knowing twinkle in his eyes? Had he guessed what she was thinking?

"Yes," she snapped more tersely than he deserved. She was instantly riddled with guilt, but she bit back the urge to apologize. She'd been doing that too much the past few days, making excuses every

time her temper flared, trying to dismiss with nonsense the erratic behavior that could only be explained honestly by admitting to pure sexual frustration. Which of course she had no intention of
admitting to, ever.

"You okay?" he asked, studying her intently.

That was another thing that drove her crazy. He
was so blasted thoughtful, so unrelentingly considerate. He always seemed to know when she was
tired, when she needed a break, when something was
on her mind. Just the way a friend would, she
thought sourly.

"I'm fine," she said, trying for a more even-
tempered tone. "Just distracted."

"Let's take a break," he said at once, regarding
her worriedly. "I could use a milkshake. How about
you?"

"A milkshake sounds good." Anything that
would get him out of the store for a few minutes so
she could gather her wits.

"Come with me. You can visit with Sharon Lynn
for a bit. She asks about you every time I go into
Dolan's to get something. She's complaining that
you're right next door and you never drop by."

There was a good reason for that, Trish thought.
Sharon Lynn was a direct pipeline to the rest of the
family. The less Trish saw of her, especially in
Hardy's company, the better.

"Not this time," she said. "I have things to do."

"What things?" he asked, deliberately testing
her.

"Things," she declared more emphatically.

He chuckled. ''Darlin', you're going to have to be more specific than that or Sharon Lynn will think you don't like her.''

''I like her just fine. And you don't have to tell her that I'm doing *things,* just that I'm busy.''

Hardy's gaze narrowed. ''I think I'm beginning to figure out the problem. You don't want her to see us together. Is that it?''

''Of course not.''

''Oh, I think it is. Because if she sees us together, she'll draw all sorts of wild conclusions, report them straight back to Harlan or the others and, *bam,* we'll be right back where we started.''

Trish sighed at his perceptiveness. ''Bingo.'' Why did the man have to have so many admirable traits? Why did he have to be perceptive, of all things? Men were usually clueless. When she'd thought of him as nothing more than a handsome, sexy scoundrel, they'd both been better off.

He tucked a finger under her chin and forced her to meet his gaze. Her skin tingled, even from such a simple touch, and Hardy looked as if he'd been singed. Still, he gazed at her evenly, his expression serious.

''Surely we can behave for fifteen minutes,'' he teased. ''I won't kiss you senseless in front of her, the way I do at least ten times a day in here, when we're all alone. I will keep my hands to myself. She won't suspect a thing.''

Trish chuckled despite herself. ''Okay, I suppose we don't have to give her anything to report back to the army of meddlers. In fact, it might be good if we're seen out in public doing absolutely nothing romantic or personal.''

"I'll even let you pay for your own shake, so no one will think it's a date.''

"Fine. I'll get my purse.'' She glanced at him worriedly. ''You are going to put on your shirt, aren't you?''

He shot her a look of pure innocence. ''Me being half-naked doesn't bother you, does it?''

"Of course not,'' she lied, perfectly well aware that he'd deliberately chosen the word *naked* just to rattle her. She refused to let him see that she was suddenly awash in images of him without a stitch of clothing from head to toe. Keeping her voice cool, she said, ''But you'll freeze if you step outside like that, and besides, I'm pretty sure Dolan's has a shirt-and-shoes policy.''

Good, sound, rational reasoning, she thought. Hardy laughed.

"Then by all means, let me grab my shirt,'' he said, his eyes twinkling with unabashed amusement.

Five minutes later they strolled next door. At two-thirty, the lunch counter was deserted. Sharon Lynn was scrubbing the grill. She brightened when she saw them.

"Oh, am I glad to see you,'' she said. ''I can take a break. I hate this job. It's one of those necessary evils I can't seem to make myself foist off on the part-time help. Are you here for food, sundaes, what?''

"Milkshakes,'' Hardy told her. ''Thick, chocolate for me.''

"Make that two," Trish said.

"How's the work coming on the store?" Sharon Lynn asked as she put double scoops of chocolate ice cream and milk into the metal container and attached it to the machine that would stir it into an old-fashioned, thick, frothy shake.

"The shelves should be done this week. I'm expecting my book order on Monday. I figure I'll be open by the first of March," Trish told her. "I thought I'd have some sort of grand opening party."

"Let me do the food," Sharon Lynn volunteered. "I can fix things other than burgers and fries. I'd love to do it. There are days when I'd kill to be able to make pretty little hors d'oeuvres."

"Work up a menu and a price list and you're on," Trish said.

"No price list," Sharon Lynn said. "The Adams family will pitch in. It will be our grand-opening present."

"I can't let you do that," Trish argued.

Sharon Lynn exchanged a look with Hardy. "Tell her," she commanded.

"It won't do you any good to argue," he said. "They're a stubborn bunch."

Trish heaved a sigh. "So I've noticed."

Sharon Lynn beamed. "Good. That's settled. I will let you okay the menu, though, in case there's anything you absolutely hate. Do you want Tex-Mex? Something more formal?"

"I'll trust your judgment. Whatever will bring the most people out."

"This time of year, when winter boredom has set

in, you could get them out for chips and dip,'' Hardy said.

"I think I can do better than that," Sharon Lynn said, grabbing a pad of paper, a pen and moving out from behind the counter to sit beside Trish. "Okay, let's decide on a theme. How about English tea? Doesn't that sound perfect for a bookstore? You could do it on a Sunday afternoon."

"I love it," Trish said, enchanted. "That's exactly the sort of atmosphere I want to create."

"Tea?" Hardy echoed disdainfully. "Itty-bitty sandwiches? We're talking cowboys here, ladies. Big appetites."

"He has a point," Sharon Lynn said.

"Then we'll have lots of itty-bitty sandwiches," Trish said. "And scones and cakes."

Hardy's expression brightened. "Cakes? Personally I like chocolate with fudge icing."

"Petits fours," Trish informed him, enjoying the way his expression fell. "Itty-bitty individual cakes," she added for emphasis.

"Girl food," he declared, dismissing it.

"Women buy more books than men," she pointed out. "Why shouldn't I cater to their tastes?"

"Yoo-hoo," Sharon Lynn said, waving a hand between them. "Remember me?"

They stared at her as if they'd forgotten her existence. Trish barely restrained a moan. This was exactly what she'd hoped to avoid. She and Hardy had been so busy arguing with each other, Sharon Lynn might as well have been on the moon. And

Sharon Lynn knew it, too. The knowing sparkle in her eyes was proof of it.

"I think we can update the tea idea a bit to satisfy the male appetites," she told Trish. "I'll make a more substantial filling for some of the sandwiches, maybe some little ham biscuits or even miniature barbeque buns."

"Better," Hardy agreed.

Trish scowled at him. "I'm so delighted you approve."

"Regular cake, too," he said, ignoring her and appealing directly to Sharon Lynn. "Sliced thick, with lots of frosting."

"I hate to say it," Sharon Lynn said, "but knowing the men in my family, they'd go along with Hardy on this one."

Trish recognized when she was beat. "Okay, regular cake, then."

"What about beer?" Hardy asked.

"Not on your life," Trish declared. "Champagne, maybe. Sharon Lynn, what do you think?"

"Let's stick with tea. It will be Sunday afternoon. We'd better do both hot tea and iced, though. I can't see these clumsy men balancing little tea cups in their hands while they shovel cake into their mouths. The phrase *bull in a china shop* comes to mind."

"Hey," Hardy protested. "Men are not clumsy."

"I still think we'd better not risk Granddaddy Harlan's best porcelain, which I intend to borrow for the occasion. He's the only one who has enough for a huge crowd." She made another note on her paper, then turned back to Trish. "What about invitations?"

"Since you two seem to be caught up in party planning, I think I'll go back next door and get some work done," Hardy said.

To Trish's discomfort, he gave her shoulder a quick, friendly squeeze before he left. Naturally Sharon Lynn caught the affectionate gesture. No doubt her imagination would run wild.

"You two seem to be getting along well," she observed, her gaze fixed on Trish's face.

"Well enough," Trish said. "About the invitations—"

Sharon Lynn cut her off, her expression alight with curiosity. "What have you two been doing all day long over there?"

"Working," Trish said, not even trying to hide her impatience. "What else?"

"Besides that?"

"Nothing," Trish declared very firmly. "There's a lot of work to be done."

"Nothing?" Sharon Lynn regarded her with a mix of disbelief and disappointment. "I thought for sure by now..." Her voice trailed off.

Trish shrugged. "Sorry. Now about those invitations, how many do you think I should have printed?"

She finally managed to drag Sharon Lynn's attention back to the task at hand. By the time she left an hour later, they had worked out most of the details for the grand-opening party. She was also pretty sure she had managed to squelch any speculation that she and Hardy were a hot item.

As she opened the front door of her store, she heard voices from the storeroom. Male voices. One, of course, was Hardy's. The other was... She listened more intently, recognized the familiar lazy drawl and almost turned around and dashed right straight back out of the building. Before she could, Hardy came in, caught sight of her and called out.

"Hey, Trish, look who's here."

Her stomach knotted as her oldest brother followed Hardy into the room.

"Dylan, what are you doing here?" she demanded tightly. "How did you find me?"

A grin spread across his face, despite the lack of welcome. "I'm a private detective, Sis. Finding people is what I do."

"Well, go find somebody else. I don't want to be found," she said, stubbornly refusing to walk into his embrace.

Dylan was as close to a rebel as any male in the Delacourt family had been allowed to get. Disgustingly handsome and fully aware of it, he'd left a trail of broken hearts in his wake until he'd met his wife and she'd turned around and left *him* with one, taking their son right along with her. Dylan had balked at going into the oil business. After listening to his father rant and rave for months, he'd gone right ahead with his own plans for his life. He, of all of her brothers, should have understood why she'd needed to get out. Obviously he didn't because he was here, probably intent on dragging her home again.

His expression softened. "I haven't told Dad where you are," he said quietly. "This is just between us."

Hope spread through her. "You swear it?"

"Cross my heart."

Then she did fly into his embrace. "I've missed you, Dylan. I would have called you, but I didn't want you to get caught between Dad and me."

"When have I ever been scared to take a bunch of garbage from Dad?" he scoffed.

"I didn't want you to because of me." She turned to Hardy. "Have you met?"

"We've met," Hardy said.

"For a minute I thought he was going to take me on, until he realized I was your brother and not Jack the jerk." He gestured at the work they'd accomplished. "I like it. It's going to be even better than the store in Houston."

She nodded. "I think so, too."

"Look, why don't you two go on?" Hardy suggested. "I'm sure you have a lot of catching up to do. I'll finish and lock up here."

"Only if you'll join us for dinner," Dylan said. "Is there someplace close we can go?"

"I'm sure Hardy already has plans," Trish said hurriedly. She didn't want her big brother getting any ideas about her and Hardy. He could be as much of a nag as an Adams. "Besides, I want you to come out to the ranch and see your niece."

"Another time," Hardy said. "Once you get a

look at little Laura, you won't want to leave her. I guarantee it.''

"A real beauty like her mama, huh?" Dylan said.

"Pretty as a picture from the moment she was born," Hardy said. "I ought to know. I was there."

Trish knew he had said that deliberately, that he was staking his claim on the two of them so her brother wouldn't mistake it. Not that Dylan was likely to go more than a minute without plaguing her with questions about Hardy, anyway.

"I'll explain on the way," she said, drawing Dylan toward the door, even as she shot a scowl over her shoulder at Hardy. Obviously unintimidated, he winked.

"Nice to meet you, Dylan. I hope to see you again before you go."

"Count on it," Dylan said, regarding him speculatively.

Trish dragged her brother out of the store. "Where's your car?"

"Across the street. Where's yours?"

"At the ranch. Hardy drove me in."

He waited until after they were in his sports utility vehicle before he glanced over at her and asked idly, "So what's going on between you and the cowboy?"

She seized on the label, rather than answering him directly. "How do you know he's a cowboy?"

"He told me. He said this work for you is just some temporary gig his boss set up."

"Exactly."

"Now that that's out of the way, why don't you tell me what's going on between the two of you?"

"Nothing," she said flatly.

"Look, Patricia Ann, you might be able to fool some people with the innocent act, but not me. There were enough sparks in that room just now to light up Houston."

"Don't be ridiculous."

"Okay, let's try this another way. Why did you decide to stay in a town like Los Piños?"

"I like it here," she said with a touch of defiance.

"What is it you like?" he persisted patiently.

The persistence and the patience were both traits that served him well as a private eye. As a brother, they made him damned annoying.

"The people," she said tightly. "Everyone here has been wonderful to me."

"Including this Hardy person."

"Yes, of course. He's been very helpful."

"How did you meet?"

She scowled at him. "Is this really necessary? I am not some criminal you're cross-examining."

"No, you're my sister, which makes this personal. How did you meet?"

She sighed. "I was stranded on the side of the road New Year's Eve. He came along."

"And?"

"I was in labor," she finally ground out. "He delivered Laura."

Dylan's eyes widened. "Well, well, well. Isn't that interesting? No wonder he's so attached to your daughter. I assume he's single."

"An inveterate playboy," she acknowledged, hoping the description would be enough to tell him why Hardy would never be a serious candidate for a husband.

Dylan didn't seem convinced. "You sure about that, sis? He struck me as a solid guy. He obviously cares about you and the baby."

"He's been very kind. And he's definitely a decent guy, which is why we have agreed that we will be friends and leave it at that."

Dylan turned and stared at her as if she'd calmly announced a decision to fly off to Mars. "You've agreed to be friends?"

"Yes."

A grin tugged at the corners of his mouth. The grin spread, displaying the devastating dimple that drove women crazy. "Oh, Sis, you are in such deep trouble."

"I beg your pardon?"

He regarded her patiently. "Men and women do not agree to be just friends, unless they're fighting the urge to be a whole lot more."

She frowned. "And you would know this because...? Is it your vast success rate with members of the opposite sex? Or the psychology degree you apparently received without me knowing about it?"

"Experience," he insisted, still chortling with glee at what he viewed as her self-deception. "I've reached a few of those agreements myself. Meant 'em at the time, too. Bottom line, though? They're not worth the time they take to spew the words out. In fact, the opposite is true. Once you've declared each other off-limits, the attraction escalates. Label something forbidden and everybody wants it. That's human nature.''

"Thank you, Dr. Ruth." She was very much afraid he was right. She certainly hadn't been able to stop thinking about Hardy in a sexual way since she'd made the decision to keep things strictly platonic. In fact, the whole friendship thing was making her a little crazy.

"Just how bad do you have it for this guy?" Dylan asked.

"I don't. We're just friends," she said one more time as if repetition would make it true.

Her brother shrugged. "Fine by me, if that's the truth. Probably just as well, too."

Her gaze shot to his face. He was staring out the windshield, his gaze locked on the highway, his expression suddenly way too innocent. "What do you mean, it's probably just as well?"

"Dad would hate him."

"Why on earth would he hate him? He's a fine man, better than Jack the jerk, by a long shot."

"But he's not an oilman. He can't be heir apparent to a vice presidency in the family business."

"Neither are you, but he tolerates you."

"I'm blood. He can't wish me away."

Trish waved off the whole discussion as absurd. "It doesn't matter. They'll probably never even meet."

Dylan's expression sobered at last. "Then you don't intend to tell Dad where you are?"

She sighed. "Sooner or later I suppose I'll have

to. I'm amazed his private detectives don't already know where I am. After all, you found me.''

"I'm better than most of those goons he keeps on staff. They're better at white collar crime than chasing wayward daughters.''

"How did you find me?''

"It was pathetically simple, really.''

"How?''

"You transferred your money from your bank account in Houston to the bank here.''

Trish groaned. "I'm obviously not career criminal material.''

"Thank the Lord.''

"You are going to keep this a secret, right? You promised.''

"On two conditions.''

"What?''

"You check in with me regularly.''

"Done.''

"And you keep an open mind about the cowboy.''

So, they were back to that again. "Why are you pushing so hard to make something happen between us?'' she asked, genuinely puzzled. Dylan had never been prone to counseling her on her love life before.

"Because I saw the way he looked at you, Sis. It's not something you should ever take for granted.''

She caught the shadows in his eyes and realized he was thinking of Kit, the woman who'd stolen his heart and then shattered it. Or if not of his ex-wife, then definitely of his son. Dylan missed Shane terribly, but he refused to admit it.

"Kit was a witch," she declared fiercely.

"No," he said just as vehemently. "I took her for granted. I neglected her. It was my fault she walked out. It took me a long time to admit it, but that's the God's honest truth."

"Then go after her, Dylan. Get her back, if you still love her."

"Too late. She got married again last week. I let her and the new hubby get full custody of Shane."

Trish was shocked and filled with pity. She knew what a terrible sacrifice her brother was making. She even thought she could understand why he'd made it. Dylan wouldn't want his son torn between two fathers. "Oh, Dylan, I'm so sorry."

He shrugged. "Too bad these brilliant flashes of self-awareness come too late. Don't you sit around until it's too late, Trish. I'd give anything to have my baby back and somebody who looks at me the way your cowboy looks at you."

"You will," she promised him. Maybe she'd go about finding the perfect candidate herself.

No sooner had the thought occurred to her than she realized that she'd been around Adamses way too long. She had four bachelor brothers and she was in serious danger of catching the matchmaking fever that seemed to be contagious in Los Piños.

Chapter Eleven

Hardy couldn't sleep. He kept thinking about the unexpected arrival of Trish's brother. He wasn't sure which of them it had shaken more, him or Trish. For Trish there had been the fear of discovery. For him it had meant the possible end to having her to himself. It had meant Laura's father might be only hours or days away from finding her, as well.

Trish claimed to want nothing to do with Jack Grainger, but when she was face-to-face with her daughter's father, would she be able to resist? Especially with her own father pressuring her?

When the stranger had first walked into the store asking for Trish, Hardy's muscles had tensed. His stomach had knotted. He wasn't crazy about the idea of any man that good-looking having a claim on her.

For five minutes, maybe longer, the possibility that he'd been the father of her baby had eaten Hardy up inside until Dylan Delacourt had finally gotten around to introducing himself.

Once Trish had turned up, some sort of mental telepathy had been exchanged between brother and sister. After that Dylan's gaze had turned speculative. He seemed to be sizing up Hardy as if he guessed that Hardy might be more than the man who was helping her build the shelves for her store. Since Dylan had suggested dinner, Hardy figured he'd either passed muster or that further interrogation was required.

Hardy wasn't entirely sure how he felt about that. He figured he already had too many people passing judgment on how he and Trish matched up as a couple. They'd been under scrutiny and under pressure since day one. For two people who had vowed to avoid marriage like the plague, it amounted to a whole lot of unwanted interference.

After Trish and Dylan had left for the ranch, Hardy had spent the evening putting the finishing touches on the shelves. He hadn't much felt like going back to the bunkhouse and enduring the inevitable teasing about his recent lack of a social life and the taunting speculation about what it meant.

Nor had the prospect of going to any of his usual haunts appealed to him. Not one single name from his little black book popped into his head. The only woman he wanted to spend the evening with was otherwise occupied. Everyone else seemed like a poor substitute. It was pathetic. What the hell was happening to him?

With the last of the shelves built and ready for the books that would be arriving any day, he had turned his attention to the floor. He spent another hour with the sander, then polished the wood until the old planks gleamed.

When he was through, he'd stood by the front door and studied the bookstore. As a child he hadn't spent a lot of time reading books, and those he had read had been borrowed from a library. As an adult, he'd never found the time either. He could see, though, how a place like this would be appealing. There was an inviting warmth to it, a hominess, a personal charm that was all Trish.

In fact, he could imagine curling up in one of those big chairs Trish had found and recovered with bright chintz. He could practically feel her settled in his lap, a beer in his hand, a glass of wine in hers, as the fire flickered cheerfully. The image aroused him as none of his past conquests ever had.

He'd finally left the store after ten, exhausted and frustrated but pleased, as he anticipated Trish's reaction when they arrived in the morning and she discovered all that he'd accomplished in her absence. The work was all but over now. Soon he'd be back in the saddle and working at White Pines. His only contact with Trish would be by chance unless something changed.

Back at the bunkhouse, he'd crawled into bed, then tossed and turned for an hour before finally giving up and going outside. Maybe a walk would settle his nerves and wipe out the thoughts that kept churning no matter how hard he tried to shut them off.

He automatically gravitated toward the creek. Even in winter, he found solace in the fast-moving water and rustling of the wind. On a night like tonight, with a full moon and a sharp nip in the air, there was something almost magical about it.

As he neared the water, he thought he heard the soft whisper of crying. Slipping quietly through the shadows, he walked toward the sound, then halted at the sight of Trish, sitting on a boulder, her knees drawn up, her coat wrapped tightly around her. She looked so dejected, so completely lost and alone, it almost broke his heart.

He stood there forever debating what to do. Obviously she had come here to be by herself, to sort out whatever demons were troubling her after her visit with her brother. Maybe Dylan had tried to convince her to go home, Hardy thought, and mentally cursed the man. Hardy might not know exactly what he wanted from Trish, but he did know he didn't want her leaving. Even in such a brief time, she had become a part of his life. Little Laura had stolen his heart.

Whatever had brought Trish here tonight, though, he had the sense that she wouldn't welcome him catching her at such a vulnerable moment. He settled for remaining out of sight, watching over her until she decided finally to leave, then following at a discreet distance as she made the long walk back to Kelly and Jordan's. Only when she was safely inside, did he go back to his own bed, where he finally fell into a restless sleep.

In the morning Hardy felt as if he'd been on an all-night bender. It was a sensation he was familiar with but this time had done nothing to deserve. That made him irritable.

When he got to Jordan's ranch, he pounded on the front door as if that carved oak barrier had offended him.

"What on earth?" Kelly demanded, when she opened it. "Hardy, is something wrong?"

He winced, then shook his head. "Sorry."

"Come on in and have some coffee. You look as though you could use it."

"No, thanks," he said, well aware that he wasn't fit company. "I'll wait in the car."

"It could be a long wait. You might as well come in. Trish isn't quite ready. She had a rough night last night, and Laura's been fussing since way before dawn."

It was the mention of the baby that got to him. "Where is she?"

Kelly regarded him with amusement. "Laura? In the kitchen in her bassinet, squalling up a storm. She seems to be unhappy about everything today. Maybe she's catching on to her mother's mood. Trish has been distracted and sad ever since her brother left."

"Let me have a try at settling Laura down," he said, already heading in that direction. He could hear the pitiful wails before he was halfway down the hall. When he reached her, she was red-faced and waving her tiny fists in the air as if to protest being neglected.

"Come here, angel," he murmured, picking her up and settling her against his shoulder. The scent of baby powder and the feel of her soft flannel blanket wiped out the last traces of his lousy mood. He patted her back. "Are you having a tough day?"

As if she understood that she finally had a sympathetic audience, her cries trailed off. Hardy grinned as she hiccuped once, then again, then finally uttered what sounded like a tiny sigh.

Trish walked in just then, looking almost as frazzled as her daughter. Her eyes weren't red from crying, but they were shadowed with exhaustion.

"Aren't you a miracle worker?" she muttered, sounding more annoyed than grateful.

"Hey, I can't help it if she likes me."

"Maybe not, but I'm sure you're thrilled to have another female conquest you can claim."

He studied her intently, trying to guess where the hostility was coming from. "Bad night?" he inquired finally, as if he hadn't already witnessed part of it and heard about the rest.

She sighed heavily and looked vaguely contrite. "Bad enough," she admitted. "I don't think she slept for more than fifteen minutes at a time. She didn't want to be fed, didn't need to be changed. I was at my wit's end. Sorry if I was taking it out on you."

"I can handle the occasional short-tempered mood. I've had my share. Ask Kelly. I almost broke the front door this morning, before she wisely got it out of my way."

She studied him quizzically. "Why?"

"Not enough sleep, too many crazy thoughts running around in my head." He shrugged. "General contrariness."

"Aren't we a pair, then?" she said, finally mustering a halfhearted smile. "I guess Kelly will be thrilled to see the last of us."

Kelly appeared at precisely that moment. "Not until you've both had a proper breakfast. Something tells me neither one of you has eaten. That's probably why you're acting like a couple of grouchy old bears."

She added something under her breath that Hardy couldn't quite catch. "What was that?" he asked, all but certain he already knew. If he'd guessed right, Kelly Adams was a very intuitive woman.

Trish's cheeks turned bright pink. Kelly beamed at him. "Not a thing."

He looked at Trish. "What about you? You heard her."

"I never heard a thing," she insisted, avoiding his gaze.

He held Laura out in front of him. "What about you, sweetness? Did you hear her?"

The baby gurgled something he couldn't interpret. "Hmm, not talking. Must mean all the women intend to stick together. Guess it had something to do with sex." He gazed into the baby's eyes. "Was that it? Was she blaming our foul moods on sexual frustration?"

"Hardy!" Trish protested, as Kelly chuckled, pretty much confirming his guess.

"Sit," Kelly ordered, putting two plates piled high with pancakes in front of them. She reached for Laura. "I'll take her now. You eat."

Hardy knew better than to argue. Even if he hadn't been starving, he would have eaten every last bite of those light, fluffy pancakes. Sweeney's flapjacks were as tough and heavy as rubber. Trish, however, toyed with hers, taking no more than a bite or two before finally pushing the plate away. Kelly studied her worriedly, then cast a helpless look at Hardy.

"Trish, you want something else?" he asked. "Maybe a banana."

"No. I'm not really hungry."

"You have to eat. You've just had a baby."

She scowled at him. "Don't you think I know that?"

"Is this that post-partum blues stuff they talk about on TV?" he asked.

Trish stood up. "No, what it is is none of your business."

She bent down to give Laura a kiss. "I'll see you later, darling girl." She managed a smile for Kelly. "Thanks for breakfast."

"No problem. You two have a good day."

Hardy added his thanks to Kelly, then followed Trish, who was already out the front door and halfway to his car. He waited until he had the car started and the heater going before he finally glanced over at her.

"Mind telling me what's really going on?" he asked gently, determined to get to the bottom of her dark mood. Like Kelly, he was all but certain it had something to do with her brother's visit.

"It's my problem. I'll work it out," she said stiffly, huddled by the door.

Hardy decided to tackle it indirectly. "How did your visit go with your brother?"

"Great. It was wonderful to see him."

He thought she sounded more glum than happy. "You two seem close."

"We are." She actually managed a smile. "Dylan's the oldest, and I'm the baby, so he's always been outrageously protective of me. At the same time, he's the only one who ever seriously rebelled against our father. He's the only one who can completely understand why I left."

"And he's going to keep quiet about where you are?"

"He promised he would."

"Did he go back last night?"

She nodded.

"Is that what's gotten to you? Are you regretting not going with him? Are you sorry you're cut off from your family?"

"No, absolutely not," she said at once. "I mean, I wish Dylan had stuck around longer. He was great with Laura. She must really like men, even at her tender age. She settled down for him, just the way she does for you."

The observation left Hardy feeling vaguely disgruntled without totally understanding why. Surely he couldn't be jealous of Laura's uncle. Did he want to be the only male she responded to, just the way he wanted to be the only male in her mama's life? Apparently.

Trish gazed at him with blatant curiosity. "Dylan seemed to like you. Believe me, that has to be a first. He hasn't had a lot of use for most of the men I know. What did you two talk about yesterday before I showed up?"

"This and that," Hardy said. He figured Trish would be mortified if she knew her big brother had subjected him to a cross-examination worthy of Perry Mason.

"I suppose he demanded details about our relationship," she said with a resigned sigh. "Dylan scared off almost every guy I ever wanted to date in high school with the macho big brother routine. Too bad it didn't work on Jack. It probably would have, if Jack hadn't been fully aware that he had my father in his corner."

"I wasn't scared off, either," Hardy assured her. "I just told him we were friends."

"So did I. He didn't believe me."

"That's his problem."

She slanted a look his way. "We are just friends, aren't we?"

It seemed to him she sounded a little plaintive, a little regretful. "That was our agreement," he acknowledged.

"And you always honor your word, right?"

"Absolutely." He glanced at her. She looked

downright forlorn. "You aren't having second thoughts, are you?"

"About being friends? No, I suppose not."

Something in her tone alerted Hardy that she was not being entirely honest here. He decided it was worth pursuing. "Because if you were to change your mind, if you did want to go out sometime on a date, it would be okay with me," he said in what was probably the understatement of his lifetime.

He turned just in time to catch her frown.

"You don't have to sound so blasted thrilled about it," she muttered.

"Actually, I would be," he said. "Thrilled, that is."

Her gaze narrowed. "You would?"

He figured he was treading on thin ice here. She wasn't exactly doing cartwheels over the prospect of dating him. He couldn't afford to put his heart on the line, didn't even know if he wanted to. He just knew things weren't working out the way they'd been the past couple of weeks. There was too much sizzling tension in the air when they were together. The only way it was likely to die down was if they did something about it.

"Sure. Why not?" he said as if it were of no consequence.

She seemed to be struggling with indecision. "Okay, we could have dinner sometime," she said at last, then hurriedly amended, "If Laura can come along, of course."

Hardy fought a grin. "She's awfully small to be a respectable chaperone," he pointed out.

"That is not why..." she began, then let her voice trail off. "Okay, yes, I did think having another person along would keep things from getting, you know."

"Too intense? Too intimate?"

"All of that," she agreed.

"Darlin', something tells me things could get intense between the two of us in a room filled with half the town."

She regarded him glumly. "Yeah, I'm afraid of that, too."

Hardy would have chuckled, but something told him he ought to be satisfied to count his blessings. Trish finally trusted herself—and him—enough to go out with him. Now why did that make him so blasted nervous?

He had perfected the art of dating by the time he was fourteen. He couldn't even count high enough to calculate the number of dates he'd been on. Showing a woman a good time was as natural to him as breathing.

But Trish was different. A date with her actually mattered. He didn't want to blow it, didn't want to come on too strong. Didn't want to do anything from which there would be no turning back.

Oh, he was losing it, all right. He was staring straight into something every bit as frightening as the jaws of death and preparing to jump right in. In fact, he was damned eager to jump in, which just proved what happened when a man lost track of the rules that had kept him free. Obviously, before this big date of theirs, he was going to have to brush off that rule book and take a refresher course or he was going to be in the kind of emotional trouble he'd spent a lifetime avoiding.

Why was she behaving like a lovesick schoolgirl? Trish asked herself for the thousandth time as she dressed for her date with Hardy. She didn't have his track record with dating, but she'd certainly been to dinner and the movies enough times that the thought shouldn't have her palms sweating. She was as jittery as a teenager getting ready for a blind date. If she could have, she would have backed out, pleading a headache or anything else she could dream up.

Unfortunately she knew that Hardy would see straight through any excuse she offered. After tonight, though, she'd rarely have to see him again. The work on the store was all but done. Hardy must have worked like a demon the night before to get the shelves finished and the floor polished. She had been astounded when she'd walked in that morning and seen the full effect of all their hard work. Tears had stung her eyes and she'd had to fight the urge to throw her arms around him and give him the resounding kiss he deserved. Fortunately she'd learned that kissing Hardy was seldom an innocent act. Her body always wanted to turn it into something more. She'd settled for giving his hand a quick squeeze, then walking around to do a thorough survey of the all-but-finished store. He'd watched her intently, his expression worried, until she'd finally turned back and beamed at him.

"Oh, Hardy, isn't it the most beautiful bookstore you've ever seen?"

"I can honestly tell you yes," he said wryly. "Of course, I probably don't have nearly as much to compare it to as you do. To me it just feels real homey."

That was precisely the effect she'd been going for, so nothing he could have said would have pleased her more. A sudden vision of this being their home, with a cozy fire blazing, had her turning away as if he might read her thoughts.

If ideas like that were going to be popping into her head, it was a good thing that their time together was drawing to a close, she concluded. What little work was left she could do herself. Tonight was to be a much-deserved celebration of sorts.

And an ending, she added, feeling more depressed than she cared to admit.

She tugged on a pair of wool slacks that she could finally fasten around the middle, then pulled one of her favorite soft-blue sweaters over her head. She added an antique necklace with a scattering of tiny sapphires to dress the outfit up, then studied herself in the mirror. Casual enough, she concluded, and not bad for a woman just shedding the extra pounds she'd added with pregnancy. She was almost back to her old figure again, except for her breasts, which were fuller. She scooped her hair up into a loose arrangement of curls, held in place by little butterfly clips made of sparkling blue jewels.

Finally satisfied, she went downstairs just as the doorbell rang.

"I'll get it," she called out to Kelly.

She opened the door, then froze, mouth agape, her breath caught somewhere deep in her throat. Hardy was wearing a Western-style outfit, all in black. If she'd ever hoped for a pure rebel in her life, he personified it.

"You look..." they began in unison, then grinned.

"Gorgeous," he concluded.

"Very handsome," she said.

And then they both seemed to run out of words, as if the importance of the evening ahead had finally sunk in.

"You two have a lovely evening," Kelly said, breaking the silence as she came into the foyer, holding Laura in her arms.

"It's just dinner and a movie," Trish insisted.

Hardy said, "We will." He glanced toward the baby. "Is Laura coming?"

Trish shook her head. "I decided she'd be better off right here. It's a cold night."

"Besides, one of these days Trish will move out and take this little darling with her. I want every second alone with her I can get," Kelly declared.

Trish caught Hardy's expression, watched it darken at Kelly's words. He said very little until they were in the truck and underway.

"You planning on moving on, after all?" he asked finally.

"No, of course not," she said, surprised not only because he'd misinterpreted Kelly's remark, but because it seemed to bother him. "But I will have to find my own place one of these days. I can't impose on Kelly and Jordan forever. We agreed I'd start looking as soon as the store is up and running.''

It sounded to her as if Hardy breathed a sigh of relief.

"You might have to build," he said, his expression turning thoughtful. "There aren't a lot of houses available around here. Families tend to stick close. If you decide to buy some land, let me know. I'll drive you around. I've spotted a couple of pieces of property that might suit you.''

"Why haven't you bought one of them for yourself?" she asked.

He shrugged. "Too much like settling down, I suppose. The bunkhouse suits me.''

See, she told herself. There was absolutely nothing to fear from spending the evening with him. Hardy Jones was not a marrying man. How many times did she have to hear that before she got the message? And why did hearing it once more irritate her so?

"You don't need your own space?" she asked.

"Not really. The place I grew up never felt much like a home, so I haven't missed having one of my own. You can't miss what you never knew. What about you?''

"I suppose I always assumed I'd have a house one day, complete with a white picket fence and a rose garden like the one Janet has at White Pines. I never wanted the sort of huge mansion my folks have. It's a showplace. In fact, I think the only reason they bought it was because they figured it would be photographed every time someone wrote about my father.''

She sighed, then confessed, ''The only place I ever felt really at home was at the little cottage they had at the beach near Galveston. My mother hated it, so she would send us kids off with the house-keeper for the summer. She and my father would pay us duty visits on weekends. They never arrived before dinnertime on Saturday and they were gone by noon on Sunday. I always laughed whenever she told a reporter about their weekend getaways as if they were some romantic little adventures she cherished.''

''Do they still have that house?''

''Dylan has it now. He bought it from them, and he and my brothers go there every chance they get. I suppose it's their bachelor pad. They invite me once a year, and I'm sure it takes them a month to clean up before my visit.''

He grinned. ''If they're anything like the bachelors I know, it might take longer.''

A few minutes later they arrived in Garden City. Hardy pulled up in front of an old hotel that had clearly been restored in recent years.

''I hope this is okay. There's a great little restaurant inside and there's a dance floor.'' He studied her uncertainly. ''Sound all right?''

The mention of the dance floor set her pulse to pounding. The prospect of stepping into Hardy's embrace, of feeling his body pressed against hers rattled her so badly she could do little more than nod.

He grinned. "Good. I've heard the band does all the old-fashioned stuff. I can't promise you I can tell a waltz from a foxtrot, but I should be able to avoid stepping on your toes."

As they walked through the lobby, Trish's gaze shot to the registration desk. Of course there would be rooms upstairs. Was that why he had brought her here? Was he expecting something more out of tonight than dinner and dancing? And what about the movie they'd talked about? Maybe he'd been hoping she'd agree to watching one in bed. How many other women had he brought here and seduced? The rat! The louse! She was about to snap out some sarcastic observation when he grinned at her.

"You can forget about dragging me up to one of those rooms," he taunted.

"Me?" she all but sputtered, radiating indignation.

His grin broadened. "Oh, I know exactly what kind of ideas popped into that head of yours, but I'm not going along with it. I promised you a quiet evening, no pressure, no need for a chaperone. I stick to my word." He gazed deep into her eyes. "You can count on it."

Trish should have been relieved, should have rejoiced at the teasing declaration that she was safe with him. So why did she suddenly wish she could drag him straight into an elevator, up to a room and then strip his clothes off?

Because he had cleverly planted the idea in her head, she realized, frowning at him. No wonder he was so successful with women. Every one of them probably thought the seduction had been their idea. Well, she knew better, and now that she did, she would be on guard.

In fact, she had a few clever moves of her own. She knew how to drive a man crazy, and no one she knew deserved it more than Hardy. Dinner was going to be lovely, she was sure. But the dancing was going to be downright fascinating.

Chapter Twelve

Hardy knew he hadn't mistaken the panic in Trish's eyes when she'd spotted the registration desk and realized the implications of the fact that they were in a hotel. She'd jumped to an instantaneous conclusion that he'd brought her here to seduce her. That she thought so little of him irked him. At the same time, he'd thoroughly enjoyed teasing her about the wicked direction of her thoughts. She had been completely flustered when she realized that he'd read her mind and turned her conclusions topsy-turvy.

Of course, now she seemed dead set on making him pay. Every time he asked her to dance, she made darned sure that she fit herself so snugly against him that every muscle in his body went rigid.

Then she'd toss an innocent look over her shoulder and sashay back to the table as if she had nothing more on her mind than another bite of salad. Meantime, he was so aroused, he ached.

They'd just returned to the table after their third slow dance, when he deliberately captured her gaze and held it. The muscles in her throat worked, and she seemed to be having difficulty breathing.

"Having fun?" he inquired lightly.

"Sure," she said, her voice choked.

The music slowed again. He held out his hand. "Care for another dance?"

"Umm, not right now," she murmured. "The salad will get..." Her voice trailed off as if she realized the absurdity of what she'd been about to say.

"Cold?" he supplied. "Hot?"

"Soggy," she said emphatically.

"Nothing I hate more than a soggy salad," he agreed. "We'll wait till you're finished then."

She toyed with the lettuce for the better part of fifteen minutes before finally eating the last little bite with obvious reluctance. She finished just in time for another slow tune.

"Ah, perfect timing," Hardy enthused. He stood up before she could make another excuse.

This time, as if she'd sensed that his patience with her game had worn thin, she tried to remain a discreet distance away from him, but Hardy urged her in close, until their bodies were pressed intimately together once more. He was aroused before they took the second spin around the floor. In fact, there was so much heat being generated between them, the chef could have cooked their meals right there on the dance floor.

He gazed down into Trish's eyes and noted that her expression had shifted from alarm to something vaguely dreamy. Instinctively she snuggled a little closer.

Check and checkmate, he thought with a hint of desperation. If they weren't careful, this game was going to get wildly out of hand. And he was going to be cursing himself for that vow he'd made not to haul her upstairs to one of the rooms.

Back at the table, he glanced at his watch. If they rushed, they could still make that movie. A darkened movie theater suddenly seemed a whole lot safer and more sensible than a dance floor, unless he intended to spend the rest of the evening being physically tormented. A good action movie, that was what they needed. That way if their blood roared, if would be from the adrenaline pumping through them, not lust.

"What do you say we get out of here?" he asked before the subject of dessert could come up.

Her startled blue eyes met his. "Now?"

"We've been here longer than I realized. If we're going to make that movie, we'd better hurry."

"We don't have to go to a movie."

"Yes, we do," he said urgently.

Suddenly a knowing grin spread across her face. "Oh, really? Why is that?"

"Just because."

"Because you're scared? Because you don't trust yourself with me, after all those assurances that nothing was going to get out of hand?"

He regarded her solemnly. "Okay, darlin', we have a choice here. We can stay here and tempt fate or we can go to a movie the way we planned, share some popcorn and drive home."

"Those are the only choices?"

"That's the way I see it."

"I vote we tempt fate."

He blinked and stared. "Excuse me."

"You heard me."

"Trish, do you have any idea what you're suggesting?"

"I'm not naive," she assured him. "But I also trust you not to do anything I don't want you to do."

Hardy all but groaned. He hated having a woman announce that she trusted him. It tossed all the responsibility for keeping a tight rein on their hormones back into his lap. He scowled at her.

"If you trust me, then believe this, we need to go to a movie. Right now," he added for emphasis. He beckoned for the waiter and started tossing bills on the table.

"No dessert?" the waiter asked.

"I guess not," Trish said with apparent regret.

"We have someplace we need to be," Hardy said, as if he owed the man an explanation.

He hustled Trish out of the restaurant, through the hotel lobby and into the car, before he forgot his good intentions.

Trish glanced over at him, eyes sparkling with mirth. "I guess this means you don't trust yourself."

"You've got that right."

She reached over and covered his hand on the steering wheel. "Hardy," she said softly.

He went absolutely still at her touch. "What?"

"I knew all along I could trust you."

He faced her and sighed. "Why? How?" he asked, perplexed by her conviction.

"Because I know the kind of man you are."

"I'm a womanizer," he reminded her emphatically. He was pretty sure there was a hint of desperation in his tone, as if he were trying to remind himself of that, as well as her.

"You're kind—"

"A playboy," he interrupted, since she obviously hadn't gotten the message.

"And decent," she continued.

"A rogue," he added for good measure.

"And thoughtful."

He tried again. "I'm like Jack the jerk."

She scowled at him. "You are nothing like Jack the jerk," she insisted. "Nothing!"

Puzzled by her vehemence, he stared. "You're the one who made the comparison, after hearing my romantic rap sheet from practically everybody in town."

"That was before I knew you," she said dismissively.

"What exactly are you saying here?"

"Just what I said earlier, I trust you. I trust you not to play games with me. I trust you not to toy with my feelings. I trust you to be honest with me."

She was regarding him with such utter sincerity that Hardy had no choice but to believe her. On

some level he was absolutely humbled by her declaration. On another level, it scared him spitless. It
was the kind of fervent statement that a man had to
live up to. He wasn't one bit sure he could.

How could he be honest, when he didn't understand his own feelings? How could he not play
games, when playing games was all he'd ever done?

He met Trish's gaze, saw the warmth in her
eyes—the trust—and wondered what he'd ever done
to deserve it. He also knew he would turn himself
inside out before he would ever knowingly do anything to let her down.

Trish spent the rest of the week thinking about
her date with Hardy. He had lived up to every one
of her expectations. He had been thoughtful, sensitive and sexier than any man had a right to be. He
had also been a perfect gentleman, giving her no
more than a perfunctory, chaste kiss when he'd
dropped her back at Kelly's after the movie. Every
wildly rampant hormone in her body had protested
the slight. She had anticipated another one of those
mind-numbing, sizzling kisses. Apparently all that
talk of trust had cooled his ardor.

Which was just as well, she assured herself,
throwing herself into unpacking the boxes of books
that had arrived at the store that morning. It was
exactly what she had wanted, a pleasant evening
with no pressure.

So why did she still feel thoroughly frustrated and
cranky days later? Maybe it was because she hadn't
caught so much as a glimpse of Hardy since that

night. Maybe it was because despite all her claims to the contrary, she had enjoyed his attention, had basked in the flirting and the sexual tension that sizzled between them whenever they were in the same room.

She heard the bell over the front door ring and glanced up from the stack of books she'd been sorting. Harlan Adams filled the doorway.

"You and that boy turned this place into something real special," he declared approvingly. "Mind if I come in and take a peek around?"

She grinned because he was already inside and actively poking around when he asked.

"It is your building. I suppose you're entitled to a sneak peek," she told him.

She watched warily as he moved slowly around the store, taking in everything. He paused by a table of bestsellers, studied the jackets of several books, then nodded approvingly.

"Good selection."

"Thank you."

"You have anything in here by Louis L'Amour?"

"I've ordered everything I could. They're in one of these boxes I haven't unpacked yet."

"Good. There's nothing like a Western to relax a man at the end of a long day. Pick out a handful for me and send 'em on out to the ranch."

"What if I pick ones you've already read?"

"Probably will," he told her. "I think I've read most of them at one time or another. Still enjoy reading them. It's like visiting with old friends. You get together over the years, tell the same old tales, laugh at the same jokes, but there's something satisfying in the repetition and in the sharing.''

Trish wished she had old friends to share things with. She'd lost touch with most of the women she'd known in Houston. Her brothers had been her best friends, and she was cut off from all of them except Dylan.

''You're a very wise man, Mr. Adams.''

''Harlan, girl. I keep telling you nobody around here thinks of me as anything else.''

''I feel I should be more respectful,'' she told him.

''That's because your folks raised you right. Okay, then, call me Grandpa Harlan, like the rest of your generation. Will that give me the respect you figure I should have?''

Trish was deeply touched by the offer. ''If you're sure.''

''I am. As far as I'm concerned, you're one of the family.''

''Thank you.''

He moved to one of the chairs in front of the fire and sank into it with an appreciative sigh. ''You sure you knew what you were doing when you brought these chairs in here?'' he asked. ''Seems to me like folks might take such a liking to them, they'd just stay the day.''

''That's fine with me. I like the company.''

He regarded her intently. ''I hear you and Hardy went out the other night,'' he said, broaching the subject so casually Trish almost missed the speculative glint in his eyes.

"Yes. Dinner and a movie."

"How did that go?"

"We had a lovely time. He's a very nice man."

"Poppycock!" Harlan declared. "The man's a rogue. Needs to settle down. You need a daddy for that little girl of yours and a man to look after you. Seems like a perfect match to me."

Trish's hackles rose. "I do not need a man to look after me," she said fiercely, then added, "sir."

He chuckled. "Guess that respect for your elders just about flew out the window for a second there, didn't it?"

"Well, with all due respect, I think you have it all wrong. Hardy and I are just friends."

"If that's the truth, then it's a pity," he said, studying her. "Can you swear to me it's the truth?"

"I don't see why I should have to."

He slapped his knee at that. "Whooee! That's just what I was hoping to hear. Means you can't say it with a straight face."

The last vestiges of Trish's determination to treat Harlan Adams with total respect flew out the window. Her gaze narrowed. "It's true what they say about you, Grandpa Harlan. You're a meddler."

"I am indeed. And proud of it. You look around Los Piños and you won't have a bit of trouble spotting some of my success stories. Haven't had a failure yet." He peered at her intently. "You smart enough to understand the implications of that?"

She chuckled, despite herself. "In other words, I should listen closely to what you say and take your advice, because you are very seldom wrong."

"Good girl. But you've got it just a little wrong. I am *never* wrong." He stood up. "Best be going now. I don't want to wear out my welcome."

Impulsively Trish crossed the room and gave him a peck on the cheek. "Thank you for caring, even if I have no intention of listening to a word you say."

He gave her a look of pure regret. "You'll learn. You're not the first to tell me to bug off, and undoubtedly, you won't be the last." He winked at her. "But in the end, I'm always right."

Trish was suddenly struck by the terrifying sensation that he very well might be right about her and Hardy, too. A part of her even wanted him to be.

But another part had lived through the disaster with Jack Grainger and couldn't help making the very comparisons that she'd denied so vehemently to Hardy just the other night. What if she was wrong? What if Hardy turned out to be exactly like the man who had betrayed her? Could she take that kind of a risk with her heart again?

Hardy tossed the fancy invitation down on his bunk without even opening it. He knew what it was for. Trish had invited him to the grand opening of her store, and he was pretty much duty bound to accept. Too many people would jump to all sorts of ridiculous conclusions if he failed to show up.

He supposed he could take a date and put all the matchmaking nonsense to rest once and for all. But he knew he couldn't do it. Not only wasn't there a single woman he even wanted to spend the afternoon with, but he knew it would hurt Trish if he showed up with a woman on his arm. It would be tantamount to admitting that her first impression of him had been the right one.

That was why when Sunday afternoon rolled around, he took a shower, dressed with extra care and drove into town for this shindig Trish and Sharon Lynn had planned. After all, how much trouble could he possibly get into at a bookstore opening? He doubted he'd have a single minute alone with the hostess, not so much as a second for stealing a kiss that might push him over the edge and shatter his New Year's resolution.

Hardy thought back to that night just a couple of months back when he'd been so confident that he could make it through another year as a bachelor. After all, he'd gone through most of the last thirty years on his own. He'd never once been tempted to change that.

Of course, he hadn't counted on delivering a baby, either. Who could have guessed that that simple act of rescuing a lady in distress would tumble his whole view of the world into disarray?

Before he could analyze the meaning of all that, he arrived at the store, only to realize that he'd instinctively arrived early. Maybe subconsciously he'd wanted that stolen moment alone with Trish, after all.

As long as he was the first one parked on the block, he couldn't very well hide out in the truck until the other guests started showing up. He might as well go inside and see what he could do to help.

He opened the door to chaos. Sharon Lynn and Trish were running around like crazy trying to get all the food arranged on folding tables they'd set up across the back of the store. Laura was in her carrier screaming at the top of her lungs, furious at being ignored. Trish took one look at him and latched on to his arm as if it were a lifeline.

She cast a look from him to her daughter and pleaded, "Do something. I thought she'd sleep through this, but she hasn't stopped crying. I don't have a second to pace the floor with her, not if everything's going to be ready when people get here."

"Leave her to me," he soothed. "Looks to me like you and Sharon Lynn have everything just about ready. Laura and I will take a little walk around the place, so she can get acquainted with the business."

"Bless you," she said fervently.

"No problem." He scooped his favorite miniature person out of her carrier and settled her against his chest. "Hey, sweet thing, let's you and me go check out the children's books. Maybe we can find you a bedtime story. How does that sound?"

To his amusement, Laura gurgled appreciatively. Trish shot him a look of pure venom.

He winked. "Your mama can't stand it that you and I have a thing going," he advised the baby. "Personally, I think she's jealous."

"No, what she is, is frazzled," Trish declared, slapping a plate of fresh vegetables and dip onto the table so hard that the dip splattered. "Now look what you made me do."

"It's okay," Sharon Lynn soothed. "We just plop the plate on top of the stain and no one will notice a thing."

Hardy headed for the children's books to get out of the line of fire. He figured if he weren't careful, the next plate was likely to end up in his face.

Unlike the huge chairs in front of the fire, the only chair in the children's section was meant for someone about a quarter of his size. He managed to scrunch down on it, while he selected a board book that looked as if it was about Laura's speed.

"Goodnight Moon," he said, reading the cover. "Sounds like a winner to me." He held it up for Laura's approval. He took her gurgles for a yes. He turned the thick pages slowly, reading to the baby and showing her the pictures. He was pretty much engrossed in the simple story when he heard the front door open and close, followed by a hoot of masculine laughter.

"Will you look at that?" Harlan Patrick said. "The world's most dedicated bachelor has taken to reading stories to the baby."

"Can this bachelorhood be saved?" Slade Sutton chimed in.

"Oh, stop it," Val ordered before Hardy could get up and silence both men with a punch. "I think it's wonderful."

"I agree," Laurie said.

Hardy felt his cheeks flame. "I was just helping Trish out. The baby was upset and she had things to do and—"

"It's okay," Val soothed. "Don't pay any attention to the two of them. They're cretins."

Slade bent down and kissed the tip of her nose. "That's not what you were saying last night."

"Last night I was deluded into thinking that you had a sensitive side," she countered.

More people flowed into the room, filling it to capacity with laughter and conversation. Slade's daughter joined them before her father's teasing could veer into dangerous territory. "Oh, she's darling," Annie cooed. "Can I hold her?"

Hardy hesitated.

"I'll be real careful," she promised.

"Over in the chair," Val instructed. "And you don't budge."

Hardy followed Annie to the chair and delivered Laura to her with some regret. "Just holler if you want me to come and get her."

"She'll be fine," Annie said, gazing at the baby with a rapt expression. She glanced up at Val. "When are you and Daddy—"

"Don't even go there," Slade said. "I'm just now getting the hang of being a father to you."

"That means you've had plenty of practice," Annie countered. "I need a baby brother or sister."

"It isn't about what you need," Val declared. "Your father and I will decide when the time is right to expand our family."

The look she gave her husband suggested to Hardy that the time was a whole lot closer than Slade suspected.

Suddenly feeling as if he were intruding, Hardy

searched for Trish in the growing mob scene, then moved off in her direction. She was standing apart from the crowd, looking a little shell-shocked by the sheer number of people who'd turned out for the grand opening.

"Looks like you have a success," he observed, moving to her side.

"I never had this many people turn out for my year-end sale in Houston," she said, her expression dazed. "And I gave really good discounts. I owe this to the Adamses, I'm sure. Their approval counts for a lot around here."

"No," he corrected. "You owe it to all your hard work and planning. Don't sell yourself short."

"I wasn't. It's just that this is amazing. I had no idea so many people would come. What if we run out of food?"

"Sharon Lynn made more than enough. Besides, most of these people just like getting together. The food's a bonus."

"I wonder if I should have hired a cashier for today," she asked worriedly. "Several people have wanted to make purchases."

"They'll be back. I think it's better that the party is just to show the place off." He glanced around. "It makes a good impression, doesn't it? Did it turn out the way you envisioned?"

"You know it did," she said. "Thanks to you."

"They were your ideas. I was just the muscle."

"Still, I can't thank you enough."

Her gaze met his, and he felt his head spin. "Trish…"

Whatever he'd been about to say was lost, because she stood on tiptoe and kissed him. It was the same kind of chaste peck on the cheek he'd given her when he'd taken her home on their date. Suddenly, though, he hated the polite little charade, the mockery of the passion that a kiss between them could be.

Before she could move away, he turned his head and captured her mouth beneath his. He took full advantage of her startled gasp, tasting her, savoring the shock of sensations swirling through him, the slight trembling he could feel in her.

When he finally released her, she stared at him mutely, her lips swollen, her eyes bright.

"We need to talk about this," he said tersely, all too aware that the room had gone silent and that they were being watched with evident fascination. "Later. I'll come back when this is over."

Trish nodded.

Because he didn't want to explain to anyone what had just happened—wasn't even sure he could explain it—Hardy fled.

He figured he had an hour, two at most, to get a grip on the emotions churning inside him. Otherwise, when he came back here tonight, he was going to break every vow he'd ever made to himself and to Trish.

Chapter Thirteen

Trish sensed that she and Hardy were at a major turning point in their relationship. The barely restrained lust simmering between them was about to sizzle out of control. She was no longer in control of her own reactions to him and, she suspected, he was losing his tight rein on his responses to her.

As the party swirled around her, she went through the motions of being a proper hostess. She chatted innocuously, skirted prying questions from the Adamses about Hardy's sudden disappearance, and made sure everyone ate their fill of scones and little sandwiches.

After a few minutes of forcing herself to play the role, it began to come naturally. She finally remembered the purpose of the party beyond simply showing off the store. She asked people about their book preferences, making mental notes for her next order. She queried them about other items that they wished a local store would carry and collected a whole list of ideas for a gift section.

All the while she kept track of the time, counting the minutes until the afternoon tea was scheduled to end. She knew Hardy would wait until the last guest was gone before making an appearance. Her pulse zipped as she mentally skipped ahead by an hour or so.

What exactly did he want to talk about? The kisses? The barely leashed passion? Was that something someone could sit down and discuss as rationally and dispassionately as the weather? She doubted it. She knew she couldn't. She had never before felt the out-of-control spinning sensations that Hardy's touch set off in her. She had nothing to compare them to, no idea if they were the sort of responses that cooled once they'd been allowed to rush wickedly to a natural conclusion.

Maybe Hardy, with all of his practice, could put a name to what was going on between them. But as badly as she wanted to label and identify it, so she could deal with it as straightforwardly as she paid invoices or balanced a checkbook, it irked her that he might have answers that she herself did not.

"Everything okay?" Sharon Lynn asked, studying her worriedly. "You're not too tired, are you? After all, it's only been a couple of months since you had the baby. You've been pushing yourself to get ready for this."

"It's okay," Trish told her. "I'm fine. I just have a lot on my mind."

"A lot or one particular man?" Sharon Lynn asked.

"A lot," Trish insisted.

Sharon Lynn grinned, her expression filled with skepticism. "Whatever you say, but I saw that kiss. If it had been me on the receiving end of it, I'd still be weak-kneed."

Before Trish could respond to that, Sharon Lynn patted her hand. "Don't worry. People are starting to leave. I'll stick around and help you clean up."

"No," Trish said a little too emphatically.

Sharon Lynn's eyes widened. "Someone else coming back to help?"

"No, of course not. I just meant it can wait till morning. Since I'm not officially opening until next Friday, I'll have plenty of time to put things back in order."

"Cleaning up is part of the caterer's responsibility," Sharon Lynn countered.

"But you're not a real caterer, so it doesn't count," Trish said, trumping her argument. "Don't fight me on this. You and your family have done more than enough to help out today."

"Okay. Then I'll just go and try to shoo everyone else out of here, graciously, of course."

Trish wasn't about to argue with that plan. "Thank you," she said fervently.

She forced herself to say goodbye to the last of the well-wishers. As soon as Sharon Lynn was gone, Trish brought the still-sleeping baby into the front so she could keep an eye on her. Then she sank down in a chair in front of the fireplace and kicked off her shoes with a sigh of relief.

She closed her eyes and allowed herself to savor the sweet success of the event. If half the people who'd said they'd be back on Friday came, she would do a booming business on her first day. Her first catalogue for this new location would go into the mail tomorrow. And the next day she would get her Web page up and running so that Internet orders could start coming in. By this time next week, she would have the first indications of whether her decision to stay here had been a sound one, at least from a business perspective.

On a personal level the jury was still definitely out. As if just thinking that had conjured him up, Hardy returned, pausing in the doorway.

"All clear?"

"The meddlers have pretty well vanished, content with their day's work," she said wryly.

He closed the door, then turned the lock, his gaze never once leaving her face. On his way across the room, he seemed to make himself look away, then paused by the food.

"Can I bring you something?"

"Any scones left?"

"A few. Orange, cinnamon-raisin and plain."

"One of each."

"With this fancy cream stuff?"

She grinned at his description of the very expensive clotted Devonshire cream that Sharon Lynn had

somehow tracked down. "Of course. A little rasp-
berry jam, too."

"You've got it."

He handed her a plate loaded down with the bite-
size scones. His own plate had a half-dozen little
ham and biscuit sandwiches and miniature bar-
beques. He'd even poured them each a glass of the
still-cold punch.

"You look beat," he said, studying her worriedly.

"It's a good kind of beat," she said.

"Today was a triumph, wasn't it?"

"I don't know if I'd go that far, but it did surpass
my wildest expectations."

He finished his sandwiches, then leaned forward,
his elbows propped on his knees, and regarded her
intently. "Now what, Trish? What's the game
plan?"

"Game plan?"

He gestured toward her and then the baby. "Will
you stay at Kelly's so she can baby-sit? Find that
house you talked about? Move on?"

He said the last as if he fully expected her to seize
that option, despite today's success.

"Why would you think I'd be moving on? Especially after today? This is it, Hardy. The store's
about to open. I intend to become a part of the com-
munity here. I'll probably start to look for my own
place this week."

He nodded, again with that vaguely relieved expression that she'd caught once or twice before.

"Hardy, tell me about your family." She had the

feeling that once she knew about his past, she could finally unravel the mystery of Hardy Jones.

His head snapped up. "My family? Why would you bring them up?"

"Because you never talk about them. I know you must have one. You reacted pretty violently when I brought up your mother. You mentioned your grandmother when we named Laura, but beyond that you've never said a word. Where's your father?"

"Dead," he said tersely and with no obvious sign of regret.

"And your mother?"

He shrugged indifferently. "No idea."

Trish stared at him. "You have no idea where your mother is?"

"She left when I was a kid. She took my sister with her. I haven't heard from either of them since. End of story. Can we talk about something else?"

With a sudden flash of insight Trish began to see the pattern that had been established in his life at a very early age. She wanted to talk about this, wanted to make him see that that early abandonment was probably the reason he never dated the same woman for more than a few weeks. He always wanted to be the one to go, rather than start to care and face another desertion. Suddenly she understood as she never had before why he kept asking if she intended to move on, despite all the evidence to the contrary. Her heart broke for him.

She sat forward and impulsively reached for his hand. Only when his gaze finally locked with hers did she say softly, "I'm not going anywhere, cowboy. I'm here to stay."

Rather than reassuring him, her words had him jerking away. "You can't make a promise like that," he retorted. "Things change." He struggled visibly until his temper cooled. "Life goes on."

Trish wanted to reassure him, almost pressed the point, but in the end she fell silent. Maybe she shouldn't make promises she had no way of knowing if she'd keep in the long run. She'd made a commitment to staying in Los Piños, but beyond that? Would she allow a full-blown relationship to develop with Hardy, a man who embodied all the traits she'd come to distrust in a man? Or would she, too, abandon him as too great a risk? She couldn't bear the thought of being one more in a string of women to hurt him so cruelly.

And so she stayed silent.

The only sound in the room was the crackling of the fire and the baby's soft whimpers as she finally stirred. Hardy reached for Laura before she was fully awake, settling her in his arms as naturally as if she belonged there. Only then did some of the tension in his face finally fade.

It was ironic, Trish thought, watching the two of them. Her daughter might well be the only female on the face of the earth that Hardy truly trusted, the only one he allowed himself to love. Seeing them together, some of Trish's reservations began to crack. How could she not fall a little bit in love with a man who was so obviously infatuated with her daughter, a man who'd put aside his own fears to bring her safely into this world?

"You're so wonderful with her," she said softly.

"Maybe it's because she's so beautiful, so completely innocent. It makes a man want to conquer the world just to make it safe for her. That must be what it feels like to be a real father, not the kind I had, but the kind a kid is supposed to grow up with." He met Trish's gaze. "Laura deserves a father like that."

"I know."

"Do you ever think about getting in touch with her biological father?"

"Absolutely not," she insisted fiercely. "I guess that means you'll just have to step into the role. You'll have to be her surrogate dad and do all the things that a real dad would do."

Stuck by a sudden inspiration, she added, "Her godfather. That's what you can be. Would you, Hardy? I should have her baptized soon, and nothing would please me more than to have you be her godfather. Please."

He looked tempted. His gaze, which was fastened on Laura's face, was filled with tenderness.

"I don't know," he said. "That's a big responsibility."

"No bigger than delivering her in the middle of nowhere," she reminded him.

"But this is something that lasts forever," he protested. "What if I mess it up?"

"All you have to do is love her, be there to guide her when she needs it. Please, Hardy. I'll ask Kelly to be her godmother, so you'll have back-up. And one of my brothers, too. You won't be in it alone.''

He nodded at last. ''I'd be honored,'' he said finally. He grazed a knuckle lightly over Laura's cheek, a ghost of a smile on his lips. ''You and me, kid. We're going to be a helluva team.''

In that instant Trish realized that she didn't want Hardy merely as Laura's godfather, as important as that role was. She wanted him as the baby's father. She knew she would never find a better one.

And despite the nagging doubts about Hardy's frequent-dating miles, she had a feeling she'd never find a better husband for herself. Because once a man like Hardy—who'd been on the receiving end of too many broken promises—finally made one himself, she suspected he would never, ever break it.

Hardy wasn't sure when he finally admitted to himself that he might be falling in love with Trish.

It wasn't the first time he kissed her. He'd kissed a hundred women at least, and none of them had made him think about forever.

It wasn't when she stared at him so earnestly and apologized for the way people were throwing them together. In fact, at that precise moment he recalled being just a little insulted that she hadn't seemed interested in pursuing a relationship with him.

It surely wasn't when he found her sitting by the creek with the moonlight turning her hair gold and tears streaming down her face. She'd looked so lost and lonely it had almost ripped his heart out, but that wasn't love.

No, when he thought back really hard over the few months she'd been in Los Piños, he was pretty sure he could pinpoint the precise moment when he'd realized she was going to be the one woman he'd never forget. It had happened on a lonely stretch of Texas highway, when she'd been cursing a blue streak and having a baby with only him to help. She had trusted him with something incredibly precious. Without even recognizing the feelings, he'd been a goner from that moment on.

Since she was so darned set on staying single, on proving that she could be mother-of-the-year all alone, he figured it was going to be a while longer before he got around to sharing the news of his feelings with her.

When she'd asked him the night before to be Laura's godfather, he'd been taken aback. On the one hand, he'd been honored that she would consider him a fit role model for the baby. On the other, he'd cursed the fact that she didn't see him as actual daddy material. The realization that that was where his head was had stunned him. He'd never expected to want to have his own family, never anticipated that there would be a woman who would overcome all of his emotional roadblocks and sneak into his heart.

Trish had. That she was the one who'd done it— a woman who had run out on another man, on an entire family—was equally startling. Funny how he had never blamed her for that, never held it against her but had assumed she'd had legitimate reasons for going, even before he'd heard the whole story.

Maybe he'd sold his own mother short all these years. Maybe she, too, had seen leaving as the only choice. He'd probably never know, but maybe it was time to forgive her, anyway.

He'd tried for a long time to tell himself his attraction to Trish was about nothing more than sex. She was off-limits, so naturally he wanted her. He'd lived his entire adult life making conquests, then moving on. With Trish there had been no conquest. Honor and circumstances had forbidden it, so there had been no urgency to move on. Only now, when it was too late, did he realize he'd stuck around just a little too long, and the impossible—the inevitable, probably—had happened. He'd fallen for her.

Now what, though? None of his past experiences had prepared him for this. He had absolutely no idea how to catch and keep a woman who really mattered. Charm alone wouldn't do it. Trish had pretty well made that clear. She seemed to like seeing him with the baby, which suited him just fine since there was a powerful connection between him and the little munchkin. Was it possible that the way to Trish's heart was through her daughter?

Riding out to see how the cattle had weathered the latest storm gave him plenty of time to consider his options. Or it would have if Harlan Patrick had stopped pestering him for more than five minutes at a time.

"I still can't get over that kiss you gave Trish last night," he said, bringing it up for the second time in less than an hour. "Right there for all the world to see. What were you thinking?"

"I wasn't thinking."

"Instinct, huh? Fascinating."

"Drop it, Harlan Patrick."

"Not just yet."

Hardy sighed. The first time Harlan Patrick had mentioned the kiss, Hardy had brought a quick end to the conversation by telling him flatly that it was none of his damned business. Since the topic was back again, he doubted that he could silence Harlan Patrick with another sharp retort. Obviously his friend had something he needed to say.

"Is there something you want to get off your chest?" he asked, wanting the topic over with once and for all, even if it meant answering one or two sticky questions.

"Okay, here's the thing," Harlan Patrick said. "I know it's probably none of my business."

"Damn straight."

His friend scowled, but kept right on. "It's just that Grandpa Harlan has taken a real liking to Trish. And Aunt Kelly and Uncle Jordan have taken her under their wings. I'd hate to see her get hurt."

"She's not going to get hurt, not by me, anyway," Hardy declared.

"Then that'll be a first," Harlan Patrick said. "You're not exactly known around town for your staying power. Trish isn't the kind of woman a man plays games with. Even if half my family hadn't appointed themselves as her guardians, she's got a powerful father who might have a thing or two to say about anybody who does her wrong."

"I know that," he said calmly. "I'm not worried."

Harlan Patrick studied him intently. "What are you saying? Are you telling me you're serious about her?"

"I'm not telling you a blasted thing," Hardy said. "If I have something to say, I'll say it to Trish."

Harlan Patrick suddenly cracked a grin. "Then I can tell Grandpa Harlan that his scheming is paying off? He's going to love that. He'll probably wait at least twenty-four hours before asking about the wedding date."

"You tell your grandfather if he knows what's good for him, he'll leave the timetable to me. Otherwise there might not ever be a wedding. Trish is skittish. She's been hurt. She hasn't exactly announced her undying devotion to me. The situation is delicate. Your grandfather has the tact of a sledgehammer."

"And you're any better?" Harlan Patrick scoffed. "Subtlety has never been your strong suit."

Hardy regarded his friend ruefully. The remark had cut a little too close to the truth. "I'm learning, though. I am definitely learning."

In fact, he intended to start this evening by suggesting to Trish that they take a drive around to look at some property for a house. *Their* house. Of course, he had no intention of telling her that part of his plan just yet. No point in rushing things, when the outcome was still uncertain.

Chapter Fourteen

Trish glanced up from the mountain of paperwork that was rapidly piling up on her desk just in time to spot Hardy standing in the doorway. Her heart flipped, despite her many warnings to herself that expecting too much from him was a mistake.

"This is a surprise. What brings you by?" she asked.

"I thought you might want to go for a drive."

"A drive? With all this work to do? I really can't."

"You said you wanted to start looking for your own place," he reminded her. "I had some time this afternoon, so I can take you."

She had said that, and she really did need to get out of Jordan and Kelly's hair. The fact that it was a lovely day with just a hint of spring in the air decided her. She tossed aside her pen.

"Let's do it," she said, reaching for her jacket. "Where are we going? How many houses can we see? Have you talked to a real estate agent?"

Hardy chuckled. "Here and there, no houses and no, I have not talked to a real estate agent."

"What do you mean no houses?"

"We're looking at property."

"I see. What about the real estate agent, though? Wouldn't that be more efficient? I can tell them what I want so we don't waste our time."

"We don't need a Realtor for this. I'm going to show you a few things I already happen to know are on the market."

"Here in town?"

"No. They're out a ways, beyond White Pines."

"But that's so far," she protested. "It would be much more convenient for me to be right here in town."

He shook his head. "We can worry about convenience another time, if you decide against these places. Okay?"

Something told her that this meant more to him than he was letting on. She recalled him mentioning that he'd seen some property that he loved. If only to see what sort of place appealed to him, she relented. "I'm game. Let's go."

The drive, which realistically would probably have taken her about an hour, took forty-five minutes with Hardy behind the wheel. He was never reckless, but he definitely tested the speed limits.

She figured it was a good thing Jordan's son, Justin, was the sheriff. Maybe that was what Hardy was counting on.

Or maybe he was simply anxious to get her impression of this property he was being so mysterious about.

Expecting open land or some sort of ranch, she was startled when he turned into what appeared to be a forest of pines. In actuality it was little more than a grove of the trees for which the town had been named. As they bounced over the rutted dirt road carved through it, she felt as if she'd wandered into a completely different world of strong, fresh scents and deep shade.

When they emerged, she realized that the pine trees had been at the top of a rise. Spread out below was a sea of wildflowers just coming into bloom and the same sparkling creek that wandered through the White Pines ranch. It was a pristine piece of land, as perfect as anything her imagination could have conjured up.

She turned and found Hardy studying her with an anxious expression.

"Well," he demanded. "What do you think?"

"I think it's the most beautiful place I've ever seen," she told him honestly.

His expression brightened. "Really? You're not just saying that?"

"Of course not. I can just imagine a wonderful little house built right up there at the edge of the woods with lots of windows looking out on this gorgeous view."

"A log cabin?" he suggested. "Something that fits into the scenery as if it belonged there? With a wide front porch and maybe stained glass on the door so that when the sun shines in the living room is filled with color?"

She fell into his dream, absorbed it as if every detail were already real. It wasn't her home he was talking about, but his. He was envisioning something she now knew was a far cry from what he'd had as a child. As enchanted as she was with the setting, how could she even think of taking this place away from him?

"Oh, Hardy, I think you should do it. Build a house exactly like that, right here. It will be incredible."

"No," he protested. "This place should be yours. It would be a wonderful place for Laura to grow up. She could have horses and a tree house. She could swim in the creek."

"She would love it," Trish admitted wistfully, then shook her head. "But you found it. It should be yours. I know it's the place you talked about a few weeks ago. You said there were others you could show me. Let's look at those."

"You won't even consider buying this one?" he asked, looking vaguely let down.

"No. I'll look at whatever else you know about and then I'll check out what's available in town. That would be the sensible thing to do."

He nodded. "If that's what you want," he said, not fighting her nearly as hard as she'd expected him to...as she'd hoped he would.

But there was a mysterious little gleam in his eyes that she couldn't quite interpret. Since Hardy tended to be a man of many secrets, she finally dismissed it as just being one more.

As they drove away, she cast one last look back at the land he had shown her. Even though sacrificing it for Hardy's sake had been the right thing to do, she couldn't help feeling a twinge of regret that she wouldn't be the one to build a home here. She almost wished she'd never seen it. Nothing they looked at afterward was even a poor second. In fact, she doubted she would ever find anything to compare to it.

Just as she was rapidly coming to understand that she would never find another man quite like Hardy.

Hardy bought the property that same night. He rousted the real estate agent out of bed to do it, insisting on putting his deposit down and making the deal right then and there.

Two weeks later the bank closing went off without a hitch, because of the sizable down payment he'd been able to make with all those years of savings he'd had no reason to spend.

For the next few weeks he spent every spare minute building his house. Because he'd told no one, because he wanted to do every last lick of work himself, it was incredibly slow going. It also cut into time he should have been spending courting Trish, convincing her that they might have a future together.

When the nonstop thoughts of her eventually

crowded out everything else, he finally took an afternoon off and drove into town. He stopped by Dolan's and picked up two thick chocolate shakes, then went next door.

There were several customers in the bookstore, all with armloads of paperbacks. Obviously Trish was fulfilling a need in Los Piños for new reading material. Everyone was chatting spiritedly with each other, except for Willetta who, to his astonishment, was sitting in a chair in front of the fire. Since Trish was busy. Hardy walked over to the seamstress.

"Hey, Willetta, I thought you'd be long gone by now."

"Went," she said succinctly.

"And?"

"Didn't like it. I'm back to stay."

He grinned. "There's no place like home, right?"

"Seems that way to me." She gestured around the room. "You two did quite a job in here. Hardly recognized the place."

"You aren't thinking of trying to steal it out from under Trish, so you can go back into business, are you?"

"Heavens, no. Retirement suits me just fine. I do think I might enjoy coming in here to visit with your girl on occasion. May even take up baby-sitting for little Laura if Trish moves to town."

"That sounds like a fine idea to me."

She studied the container in his hand. "What's that?"

"A chocolate milk shake. I brought it for Trish,

but I'll bet she wouldn't mind if I gave it to you, instead.''

She gave him a mock frown, even as she reached for the drink. "Can't bribe me, boy. I still intend to tell her you're a rascal every chance I get.''

"I think she already knows," Hardy confessed. "But I'm hoping she doesn't mind.''

Willetta nodded. "So, that's the way it is, is it? Nothing like a good woman to settle a man down. Have you asked her to marry you yet?''

The question had barely been uttered when Hardy heard a gasp. He turned to find Trish staring at Willetta in shock. Because Trish looked so thoroughly flustered, he winked at Willetta.

"Hush," he warned her. "She's listening.''

Willetta touched a finger to her lips. "She won't hear a thing from me.''

Of course, she already had. Try as he might, though, he couldn't get a real fix on her reaction. Was she merely surprised? Or dismayed?

Oh well, he thought. There was time enough for her to get used to the idea. He didn't intend to bring the subject up until he could show her the house he'd built for the three of them.

"Hey, darlin'," he greeted Trish as if his conversation with Willetta had been about no more than the weather. "I brought you a milk shake, but this customer of yours stole it away from me.''

"Is that so? Guess I'll just have to take this one, then," Trish said as she nabbed his drink right out of his hand in a move so smooth the slickest pickpocket would have admired it. She regarded him triumphantly as she took a long, slow swallow.

Hardy shook his head with exaggerated regret. "I had no idea the women in this town were nothing but a bunch of sneak thieves."

Willetta stood up. "Guess I'll be going now. Looks like you two have things to talk about." She patted Trish's shoulder. "Thanks for the visit. You just let me know anytime you want me to baby-sit."

"Absolutely," Trish said, then fell silent as Willetta left them alone.

Hardy noticed that she seemed vaguely uneasy as she waited for him to say whatever was on his mind. Obviously she was expecting him to jump straight into a marriage proposal. She should have known he had more finesse than that. He'd also learned a whole lot about timing through his dating years. He knew when to make his move and—up until Trish, anyway—he'd always known when to make his exit.

"Something on your mind?" he inquired, regarding her with lazy curiosity.

"Me?" She stared at him blankly. "No. I thought...I mean, Willetta..." Her voice trailed off.

"Eavesdropping?"

"Of course not!" She sighed heavily. "What brings you into town? You haven't been around for quite a while now."

"I've been busy."

"Really? Grandpa Harlan says he hasn't seen much of you at the ranch, either."

"The two of you spend much time talking about me behind my back?"

"Of course not."

He grinned at her vehemence. "Tell the truth, darlin'. Were you missing me?"

"No. I just wondered, that's all. I told him you probably had a new girlfriend."

Despite her oh-so-casual tone, she looked mad enough to spit at the prospect of him being with another woman. Maybe what they said about absence was true. Maybe it did make the heart grow fonder.

"Would it bother you if I did?" he asked innocently.

"Absolutely not," she said just a little too hurriedly. "You're free to do whatever you like."

"That's the way I see it," he agreed. Because she was beginning to look as if she might haul off and pummel him, he decided maybe he'd tormented her long enough. "There's no other woman, Trish."

"Did I say I cared?"

He chuckled. "You didn't have to. It was written all over your face."

"Well, you can hardly blame me for jumping to that conclusion, given your track record."

"I'm a reformed man. I thought you knew that."

He stood up and took a step toward her. She went absolutely still.

"Come here, darlin'," he coaxed softly.

Fire flashed in her eyes. "Why should I?"

"Because you know you want to."

She frowned at that. "I do not want to," she retorted emphatically.

"Once you're over here, you can decide then if you'd rather kiss me or smack me," he pointed out.

"Now that's an interesting suggestion," she admitted.

She crossed the few feet between them until she was so close that Hardy could feel her breath fanning across his cheek. He forced himself to wait, to let her make the choice.

Finally, after what seemed an eternity, she reached up and pressed her hand to his cheek. Hardly a smack, but not the kiss he wanted either.

"Trish?"

"Hmm?"

"I've missed you," he whispered, his voice ragged.

"I've been right here," she reminded him.

He touched her cheek, then ran his thumb over her lips. "You can't get the words out, can you?"

"What words?"

"That you missed me."

Eyes sparkling, she challenged, "Who said I did? Laura, however, is another story. She has definitely missed you."

"Has she said so?" he teased.

"No, but she fusses, and I can tell she's not happy that I'm the only one around to pick her up."

"Maybe I'll come see her tonight, if I'm invited."

Trish's gaze locked on his. "I don't know what to make of you, Hardy Jones," she said almost to herself.

"I'm a straightforward guy," he insisted.

"No," she contradicted. "You're the most complicated man I think I've ever known."

"Is that good or bad?"

Looking bemused, she admitted, "I'm still trying to figure that one out."

"Let me know when you do, okay?"

"Oh, you'll be the first to know," she assured him.

Hardy was deliberately driving her a little bit crazy, Trish concluded after his visit to the store and his brief stop to see Laura that same night. She didn't want to be falling in love with a man she couldn't figure out, but she was afraid it was too late to stop herself.

She also couldn't help wondering if that was why she'd put off finding a house in town. She'd made up a dozen excuses for not even looking. Kelly had aided her indecision by insisting that she loved having Laura with her all day, that Trish was doing her a favor by staying on and filling Kelly's "empty nest," as she put it.

But despite her inability to find a new home for herself, Trish was feeling good about her new life in Los Piños. She was surrounded by friends. Her business was already showing distinct signs that it would thrive. And Laura was getting bigger every day. At four months, she was already the delight of her mama's life, the bright spot in her days.

Satisfied that her life was on an even keel, and tired of Dylan's constant pestering, she finally decided she was strong enough to withstand her father's pressure and her mother's disappointment. She called her father at his office.

"Patricia Ann, where the devil have you been hiding out? I've had my men combing every major city in the country looking for you," Bryce Delacourt blustered when he recognized her voice.

"I thought you called them off," she chided.

"Well, of course I did, for a time. Then I started to get worried when I didn't hear from you again. Thought maybe you'd gotten yourself in trouble in some strange city."

Trish grinned when she thought of how close she really was and how her unsuspecting father had never even considered looking in such a small town.

She drew in a deep breath and admitted, "Actually I've been staying with some friends of yours."

"Who?" her father demanded indignantly. "They can't be friends of mine if they've kept your whereabouts a secret. Besides, I've called everyone I could think of to see if they've heard from you."

"I insisted that they keep quiet," she said. "I told them I would disappear if they told you. They've been doing you a favor by keeping my secret."

"What the hell kind of twisted logic is that?"

"Accept it, Daddy, or I will hang up this phone right now and you'll still be in the dark."

He sighed heavily. "Okay, okay, just tell me where you are and I'll come to get you."

"I'm in Los Piños, staying with Jordan and Kelly Adams," she confessed finally.

"Blast it all, I spoke to Jordan not three weeks ago. He never said a word."

"Because he's an honorable man and I had asked him not to. Don't blame him."

"Well, that's water under the bridge now. Get your things packed. I'll be over there to pick you up first thing tomorrow."

Trish sighed. He still wasn't listening to her. She tried again. "I am not leaving here, Daddy. Get that through your head right now. I would love it, though, if you and mother would like to come and meet your granddaughter. Her baptism will be in a few weeks. That would be the perfect time."

"I'll be damned if I'm waiting a few weeks. I'll be there tomorrow," he repeated, then hung up before she could argue with him.

She carefully replaced the receiver in the cradle, then turned to find Kelly observing from the doorway.

"Everything okay?"

"I just spoke to my father. He says he'll be here tomorrow."

Kelly nodded. "It's good that you finally talked to him," she said. "And I'll make myself scarce in the morning, so you'll have some privacy. Just remember that you're an adult. He can't make you do anything you don't want to do. You have a life here now and plenty of people who love you."

Trish squeezed her hand. "Thank you."

"Maybe you should tell Hardy that your father's coming. I'm sure he'd be glad to stick around and prevent bloodshed. I doubt many men would want to tangle with him. He might be a more than even match for your father."

Trish wistfully considered the idea, then dismissed it. "It wouldn't be fair to drag him into the middle of this. It's not his battle."

"Oh, believe me, I suspect he'd be more than willing to make it his. He has a stake in what you decide, you know."

Trish wasn't entirely sure anymore that Hardy would care one way or another what she decided. He'd made himself scarce lately, which had left her wondering. The truth was, though, that the decision to stay had been made months ago, when her feelings for a certain cowboy had taken her down a path she'd sworn not to travel. She'd worry about his feelings another time.

"No, I have to handle this on my own, once and for all," she said firmly.

Then she went up to her room and spent a restless night waiting for the fireworks to begin.

Her father arrived on her doorstep at midmorning on Sunday. Jordan and Kelly had left for church with a promise not to return until late in the day.

"Call us over at White Pines, if you need us to come back sooner," Kelly had said, giving her a kiss on the cheek before they left. "Be strong."

Trish remembered that advice as she stared first at her father, then at the man beside him. Trish wished she'd asked the Adamses to stay, after all. She hadn't expected her father to drag Jack Grainger along, rather than her mother. Obviously he hadn't given up on his scheme to see them married. She was only surprised he hadn't brought a minister along.

"I want this settled right here and right now," her father declared as if he had a perfect right to take charge. He pushed past her into the living room without pausing to give her so much as a hug.

"We'll set a wedding date today," he announced. "It will have to be a small, quiet wedding, of course. As much as your mother and I had hoped for something lavish for our only daughter, we realize we can't have a huge blowout under the circumstances."

Trish clenched her fists and stiffened her resolve. Not once did she meet Jack's gaze. "No wedding, large or small. Not to Jack," she said quietly, but firmly. "I've made a life for myself here, and this is where I intend to stay."

"You're being emotional," her father said. "Let's look at this reasonably. You and Jack have a child. You should be married and raising that child together."

"If that child is so important to you, why haven't you even asked to see her?" she shot back.

"There will be time enough after we get this settled," her father responded. He drew a pocket planner out of the briefcase he'd brought along as if this were a business meeting, rather than a reunion with his long-lost daughter. "I have a free Saturday coming up the second weekend in June. That ought to give you and your mother time enough to make the arrangements. She's already spoken to the florist and the caterer, so they're on standby."

"You're not hearing me," she said sharply. "I will not marry a man who was cheating on me when we were engaged." Her gaze clashed with her father's. "That is final."

Her father didn't seem any more surprised by the revelation than her mother had been months ago. To her fury he waved it off as if it were a minor inconvenience, no more important than a difference of opinion over how to squeeze toothpaste from the tube.

"Sowing his wild oats," he said, dismissing Jack's indiscretion as if the man weren't even in the room to speak in his own defense. "I'm sure he's sorry, aren't you, Jack?"

Without giving Jack time to reply, her father went right on trying to bulldoze over Trish's objections. Jack was beginning to look a little green around the gills, in Trish's opinion, which made her wonder what her father had done to get him here. Still, he never even tried to voice an objection. The truth was, Jack never took a stand for or against anything that mattered. Obviously he wanted that promised vice presidency too badly.

"No," Trish said again. "You're not listening to me, Daddy. This wedding is not going to happen."

Her father frowned, more at the interruption, no doubt, than her declaration.

"Forget it," she said, just to make her point one more time.

"Why are you stubbornly clinging to the past?" he demanded. "What's done is done."

"This isn't about the past," she retorted.

"Then what is it about?"

"Me," a familiar voice declared, startling all

three of them. Hardy stood in the doorway, his eyes flashing sparks. He was dressed all in black, just the way she liked him best, but there was no question about him being the hero of the hour. "It's about me. Trish is going to marry me."

Trish's mouth gaped. Jack looked relieved. Bryce Delacourt stared.

"Who the hell are you?" her father demanded.

Trish rallied, grateful that once more Hardy was there when she needed him. She knew in her heart he was the kind of man who always would be.

"Daddy, this is Hardy Jones." She took Hardy's callused hand in her own and squeezed. "My fiancé."

Chapter Fifteen

Hardy could tell that Trish thought he was just putting on an act for her father's benefit, but he'd never been more serious in his life. Standing in the doorway, listening to Bryce Delacourt's commands and watching that sleazy Jack Grainger turn greener with every word his prospective father-in-law uttered had solidified his resolve.

He'd taken one look at Laura's wimpy father and seen red. That gussied-up stranger was not going to take his family away from him. He'd lost a lot of people he'd loved, but with a sudden flash of insight, he'd realized that he didn't need to lose Trish, that he *couldn't* lose her. He'd planned on waiting until the house was finished, until he had something to offer her, but Kelly's warning about the arrival of Trish's father had spurred him into action.

SHERRYL WOODS 235

Heart pounding, he had raced all the way in from the pasture where she had found him working with Harlan Patrick. He hadn't even stopped to worry about the impression of pure desperation he was leaving with his friend and Kelly, a reaction that would no doubt be spread around White Pines by nightfall. The gossip was the least of his concern at this point.

Instead, he'd stood there trying to calm the frantic racing of his pulse, listening to Delacourt making plans for his daughter, riding roughshod over Trish's objections. All it had taken was a sign from Trish that she didn't want Jack Grainger, and Hardy had been more than eager to jump into the fray. He'd already heard her vehement protests from a hundred yards away, which made it all the more difficult to understand why her father couldn't grasp what she was saying when they were in the very same room.

Hardy stepped forward and held out his hand to Delacourt. "Sir, I'm Hardy Jones. I'm pleased to meet you. I know how much Trish respects your opinion, so I'm hoping you'll give us your blessing."

The older man still appeared stunned by the sudden turn of events, but he was too much of a businessman to ignore an outstretched hand. He finally shook Hardy's hand. "Good to meet you."

Then he turned his gaze on Trish, regarding his daughter with a mix of disbelief and resignation. "You're sure this is what you want?"

"Absolutely."

She said it with such fervor that Hardy almost

believed she really meant it. He took her hand again and gave it a reassuring squeeze.

Delacourt glanced at the once-prospective bride-groom, whose color had finally returned. "Sorry, Jack," he said gruffly. "I never meant to put you in an uncomfortable position. If I'd known what was going on in Trish's head, I wouldn't have insisted you come along."

Trish beamed at Jack, too. "I'm sure you agree that this is for the best," she told her former fiancé. "Now if you'll both excuse me. I need to go upstairs and check on Laura." She glanced at her father. "Would you like to meet your granddaughter?"

"Of course," he said, starting from the room after her.

Grainger cleared his throat. "Would you mind…could I see her, too?"

To Hardy he sounded as if it were a duty he dreaded, rather than a joy to be embraced. He dropped another notch in Hardy's estimation.

"Certainly," Trish said. "She is your daughter, Jack. Whether you play a role in her life is up to you."

"Before you go upstairs, there's one thing I'd like to say," Hardy said, needing to make his own intentions perfectly clear. He directed his gaze straight at Grainger. "Neither of you men know me, but I want you to know that I couldn't love Laura more if she were my own. I'll be the best father she could possibly have, so you can rest easy on that score."

Delacourt nodded approvingly. Grainger flushed as if he guessed that Hardy was warning him away.

And Trish stared at him, looking surprised. Apparently she still believed that his sudden appearance, his sudden claim to being her fiancé was all a generous, impetuous charade just to get her father off her back. His sudden assertion that he intended to be a good father to Laura had taken things to another level. He clearly had shaken her.

"You all go ahead. I'll be here when you get back," he said. The thought of seeing Jack Grainger with the baby made his stomach turn over. Besides, he needed some time to figure out exactly how he was going to convince Trish to actually marry him.

The three of them were gone for less than a half hour. Obviously Grainger hadn't been struck dumb by fatherly instincts at the sight of his daughter.

When they came back downstairs, Trish was carrying the baby. In a gesture that was probably meant to make a statement she promptly handed Laura to Hardy.

Grainger looked as if he couldn't wait to get away. He barely glanced at Laura before heading out the front door. Trish's father paused long enough to give Hardy a speculative look.

"I'll be in touch," he said to Hardy, then turned to give his daughter a hug. "Your mother will want to talk to you about those wedding plans."

Trish nodded, then stood in the doorway and watched him go.

As soon as Hardy and Trish were finally alone, she looked at him with that grateful expression he was coming to hate.

"Don't even say it," he muttered, beginning to pace.

"Say what?"

"Thank you."

"I wasn't going to," she swore. "I was just going to say that you don't have to go through with this. I'll figure out some way to get out of it. After things settle down, I'm sure I'll be able to come up with something. After all, it won't be the first engagement I've broken off."

Hardy swallowed back fury. Obviously she thought she had it all figured out. Well, she wasn't counting on him. He would hold her to their engagement if he had to conspire with her father and her mother to pull it off.

In the meantime, he thought he knew just how to show her that his intentions were honorable.

"We can talk about it later," he said. "I've got to get back to work."

"How did you know about my father being here, anyway?" she asked as she took Laura from him and followed him to the door. Before he could answer, she waved off the question. "Never mind. I'm sure Kelly told you. She couldn't wait to get out of here this morning. She said she had things to do before church."

"Don't blame Kelly."

"Of course not. She was trying to protect me, just like you were. I'm really—"

Hardy touched a finger to her lips. "I thought I told you not to say you were grateful. I don't want your thanks. I was here because I wanted to be, dar-lin', because I *needed* to be.''

Let her think about that for a while, he thought as he bent down and brushed a kiss across her fore-head.

"I'll pick you up tonight at six," he said. "Where will you be, here or in town?"

She stared at him blankly. "Tonight?"

"We need to talk about the engagement, remem-ber?"

For a second a shadow moved across her eyes. Could it have been disappointment? Hardy won-dered. Had she wanted to keep up the pretense just a little longer?

"Yes, of course," she said, looking vaguely un-settled. "Breaking it off. I suppose the sooner the better, so my mother doesn't have time to get too carried away with the plans."

"Definitely the sooner the better," Hardy agreed. Of course, he had an entirely different ending in mind than she obviously did.

"Six o'clock, then. I'll be here."

She sounded dismayed rather than pleased he was about to grant her a reprieve. He found that down-right promising.

Apparently Hardy couldn't even bear the thought of a fake engagement, Trish thought bitterly as she watched him drive off, then chided herself for car-ing. After all, he had been there when she needed him. That was what mattered. The rest was simply a matter of coming up with a plan that would extricate them both from an awkward situation.

So why did she feel worse about a broken phony engagement with Hardy than she ever had about losing the real thing with Jack? Because she foolishly wanted it to be real, she admitted.

"What kind of fool does that make me?" she asked her daughter.

Laura stared back at her with solemn eyes, as if she knew just how much was at stake, as if she could guess that they were about to lose the most important man in both their lives.

Feeling as if she were about to face a firing squad, Trish still forced herself to dress with care that evening. Surely she could get some satisfaction from making Hardy regret walking out on her.

When she walked downstairs in a dress that dipped and clung in all the right places, Kelly shot her a knowing look.

"I gather you intend to render the man speechless," she said lightly.

Now there was a thought, Trish admitted wistfully. If Hardy couldn't gather his wits after getting a good look at her, he couldn't break the engagement.

"Something like that," she told Kelly.

When Hardy arrived a few minutes later, he was wearing a suit. Obviously he considered the end of their engagement to be a special occasion, too, she concluded sourly.

He also seemed nervous, which wasn't like him at all. He hadn't been this ill at ease since the night he'd been forced to deliver Laura in the front seat of his pickup, or the morning after when he'd faced her again.

Rather than head toward Garden City as she'd expected, he turned in the opposite direction.

"Where are we going?" she asked curiously.

"Someplace new," he said.

Obviously he'd chosen a place where the memories of this awkward night wouldn't come back to haunt him later, she concluded.

When they neared the familiar sight of the pine woods, Trish's heart began to beat a little faster. When he turned onto that same rutted road, she shot a speculative look at him.

"This is an odd place for a restaurant," she said quietly, watching his face.

"No restaurant," he said. "I thought we ought to be someplace more private for this talk."

She supposed that was considerate, but why here? This was his special place, and now they were about to ruin it with a discussion about how to end something that had never really begun.

Just then they emerged from the woods. Trish's mouth gaped as she saw the beginnings of a house, the same beautiful log cabin that Hardy had described to her the last time they were here.

"You're building it," she whispered, delight spreading across her face. "Oh, Hardy, it's going to be wonderful. Is this what you've been up to these past few weeks?"

He nodded. "Do you really like it? It's still a long way from being finished, because I'm doing it all myself.'' He gave her a surprisingly shy look. ''Want to take a look around?''

''Of course,'' she said, already exiting the truck.

He grinned at her enthusiasm. ''Wait for me. I'll show you around so you don't trip over something.''

When he reached her side, he took her hand and led her up the front steps onto the wide porch. The front door was in place, complete with the stained-glass window. The design was obviously a custom one, because right in the middle was a bouquet of flowers and—she leaned closer to be sure—an open book.

''Hardy?'' she whispered.

''Don't say anything yet. Just stick with me.''

He drew her into what would be the kitchen, then a formal dining room, then finally into a living room that faced the field of wildflowers, the creek and the setting sun.

''It's breathtaking,'' she said over the lump in her throat.

''Then you won't mind having dinner right here?'' he asked.

''Here?''

He showed her out onto a back patio where a table had been set with the finest silver and china. Champagne was on ice in a bucket. Trish's heart skipped a beat. This was a far cry from the dismal way she'd expected the evening to go. Was it possible, could he have a different ending in mind? She wanted desperately to believe that it could be.

''You've really gone to a lot of trouble,'' she said, meeting his gaze, trying to read his expression.

"You like it?"

"Of course I do. The house, the dinner, everything. You even got the sun to set right on cue."

He grinned. "That took some planning."

"I'm touched," she said. "And grateful."

"Why?"

"I was dreading tonight."

He drew her close. "Darlin', there's nothing to dread."

"But I expected everything to end and now…" She studied him intently. "You're not going to end it, are you?"

He laughed suddenly. "You can read me like a book, can't you?"

"Not always," she admitted. "For instance, right now I can't figure out why you're keeping me in suspense."

"About?" he teased, eyes twinkling.

"Fine," she muttered. "Suit yourself. I think I'll pour myself a little champagne."

She walked over and picked up the bottle, then handed it to him to open. He popped the cork, picked up a glass and handed it to her. She heard something ping against the crystal wineglass and glanced inside. Her mouth dropped open, a lump formed in her throat.

When she could finally speak, she said, "It's a ring."

"Really? Let me see," he said, peering into the glass. "Why, so it is. A diamond, in fact. Now how do you suppose that got in there?"

She touched his cheek. "Hardy, don't," she

pleaded. "Don't play games. Not about something this important."

He met her gaze, then silently plucked the ring from the glass and held it up so that the waning sunlight made sparks shoot from it. His gaze still clinging to hers, he said solemnly, "I know we got engaged this morning, and I know you assumed it was just an impulsive thing I did to get your father off your case, but it wasn't, darlin'. I love you. I want this engagement to be real. Brief," he added fervently, "but real."

Tears swam in her eyes. "How brief?"

"Oh, I'd say a few days ought to be long enough, but you can decide. That is, if you'll agree to marry me, if you'll let me be your husband and Laura's father."

A million things crowded into her mind at once. Joy spread through her heart. She couldn't seem to think of a thing to say.

"Trish?" Hardy prodded, his expression worried.

"I'm overwhelmed," she said finally. "I'm grateful."

"Dammit, I don't want your gratitude," he said impatiently.

She kissed him to silence him. "I am grateful," she repeated. "But I was also going to say that I love you, Hardy Jones. You are the most amazing, sensitive, incredible man I've ever known."

Hardy stopped and stared, clearly taken aback. Apparently he'd expected to have to put up more of a fight. "Say that again."

"I love you," she said, grinning.

"You do?"

She nodded. "Get used to it, cowboy. Your bachelor days are numbered."

Hardy whooped and gathered her into his arms. He twirled her around until they were both dizzy and giddy.

Laughing, Trish gazed into his eyes. "I take it you're not as upset by this as you would have been a few months ago?"

"Upset? No way." He peered at her intently. "You are saying you'll marry me, right? You are saying yes?"

"No need to say it," she informed him. "I've already told the world—well, my father, anyway—that we're engaged. I wouldn't want to make a liar out of either one of us."

"No, indeed. We couldn't have that."

She regarded him seriously. "Hardy, I know you never planned on getting married or having a family. I heard all about your New Year's resolution when I first got to town."

Hardy grinned, seemingly unperturbed. "You ever know a New Year's resolution that hasn't been broken?"

"As long as you don't feel the same way about wedding vows, I'd say we're in business."

He kissed her until her head spun. "No, darlin'. Those words are the kind a man says just once, and they're meant to last forever."

Trish wanted him so badly she ached with it. "Does this house have a bedroom yet?"

Hardy swallowed hard. "Not yet. Why?"

"Because I desperately want to make love with my new fiancé."

"Is that so?" he asked, clearly intrigued. "I have a very thick, fluffy blanket in the truck and we're all alone in the middle of nowhere. How would you feel about making love right out here?"

She was already reaching for his tie. "Forget the blanket," she said at once.

"But—" The protest died on his lips, when she reached for the buckle of his belt.

His hands swept hers out of the way, then reached for her, sliding her dress over her head in one clever movement. "You never cease to amaze me," he told her.

"Think I can satisfy you after you being used to having a different woman every few days?"

"I think you can surprise me through eternity," he said, as he unclasped her bra and filled his hands with her breasts. "You are perfect."

"Not so perfect," she said, cataloging what she thought of as her many physical flaws. Hardy paid extra attention to each one she mentioned, moving from breasts to hips to thighs in a way meant to reassure her that what she saw as flaws, he viewed as sensuous, seductive parts of a whole woman, a woman he was desperately in love with.

He dragged a cushion from a chair before lowering her to the patio. No bed could have been as romantic as this impromptu one under a sky that was rapidly turning from orange to mauve to velvet.

"I have imagined being with you a thousand and

one times,'' he told her as he entered her at last. ''None of them were anything like this.''

''You probably figured we'd be in a bed,'' she teased, rising to meet the thrust of his hips, awed by the sensations rippling through her. She had never felt so full, so complete, not just where he had entered her, but in her heart.

''I should have known,'' she said on a gasp of pure pleasure.

''Known what?''

''That it would be magic.''

''We'll keep it that way,'' he promised as he began a rhythm that drove out all teasing, all thought.

Wave after wave of wicked sensations washed over her, until she cried out his name, then felt him shudder with his own powerful release.

As the stars came out, they relaxed in each other's arms.

''I guess we're well and truly engaged now,'' Trish declared, turning to face him.

He grinned. ''I guess we are.''

''No backing out.''

''I wouldn't think of it, especially since that entire box of condoms I bought in case tonight went the way I hoped is still out in the truck with the blanket. I'm sorry. We haven't even talked about having more kids.''

''I want your babies, Hardy.''

''Laura is mine, in every way that counts.''

Her heart melted at the declaration. ''I know you feel that way. It's one of the reasons I love you.''

''Are there others?''

"Too many to name in a single night," she told him, meaning it.

"That's okay, darlin'. We have a whole lifetime for you to fill me in. Then we can spend eternity with me telling you all the ways I love you and how I'll never in a million years let you get away."

* * * * *

Watch for the next chapter in the story of
The Delacourts of Texas, when Dylan gets
caught up in the search for a missing child
and falls for the boy's single mom.
DYLAN AND THE BABY DOCTOR
will be out in March 2000.

If you enjoyed what you just read,
then we've got an offer you can't resist!

Take 2 bestselling love stories FREE!

Plus get a FREE surprise gift!

Clip this page and mail it to Silhouette Reader Service™

IN U.S.A.	IN CANADA
3010 Walden Ave.	P.O. Box 609
P.O. Box 1867	Fort Erie, Ontario
Buffalo, N.Y. 14240-1867	L2A 5X3

YES! Please send me 2 free Silhouette Special Edition® novels and my free surprise gift. Then send me 6 brand-new novels every month, which I will receive months before they're available in stores. In the U.S.A., bill me at the bargain price of $3.57 plus 25¢ delivery per book and applicable sales tax, if any*. In Canada, bill me at the bargain price of $3.96 plus 25¢ delivery per book and applicable taxes**. That's the complete price and a savings of over 10% off the cover prices—what a great deal! I understand that accepting the 2 free books and gift places me under no obligation ever to buy any books. I can always return a shipment and cancel at any time. Even if I never buy another book from Silhouette, the 2 free books and gift are mine to keep forever. So why not take us up on our invitation. You'll be glad you did!

235 SEN CNFD
335 SEN CNFE

Name	(PLEASE PRINT)	
Address	Apt.#	
City	State/Prov.	Zip/Postal Code

* Terms and prices subject to change without notice. Sales tax applicable in N.Y.
** Canadian residents will be charged applicable provincial taxes and GST.
  All orders subject to approval. Offer limited to one per household.
  ® are registered trademarks of Harlequin Enterprises Limited.

**PAMELA TOTH
DIANA WHITNEY
ALLISON LEIGH
LAURIE PAIGE**
*bring you four heartwarming stories
in the brand-new series*

So Many Babies

At the Buttonwood Baby Clinic,
babies and romance abound!

❤❤❤❤❤❤❤❤❤❤❤

On sale January 2000: **THE BABY LEGACY**
by Pamela Toth

On sale February 2000: **WHO'S THAT BABY?**
by Diana Whitney

On sale March 2000: **MILLIONAIRE'S INSTANT BABY**
by Allison Leigh

On sale April 2000: **MAKE WAY FOR BABIES!**
by Laurie Paige

Only from Silhouette **SPECIAL EDITION**
Available at your favorite retail outlet.

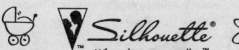

Silhouette®
Where love comes alive™

Visit us at www.romance.net   SSESMB

Start celebrating Silhouette's 20th anniversary with these 4 special titles by *New York Times* **bestselling authors**

Fire and Rain*
by Elizabeth Lowell

King of the Castle
by Heather Graham Pozzessere

State Secrets*
by Linda Lael Miller

Paint Me Rainbows*
by Fern Michaels

On sale in December 1999

Plus, a special free book offer inside each title!

Available at your favorite retail outlet
**Also available on audio from Brilliance.*

Where love comes alive™

Visit us at www.romance.net

PSNYT_R

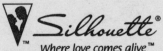